FRONTISPIECE
Zane Grey.

THE
WOLF TRACKER

AND

OTHER ANIMAL TALES

by Zane Grey

FOREWORD BY LOREN GREY

Grey, Z.

SANTA BARBARA PRESS
1984

THE WOLFTRACKER
©1924 by Zane Grey; renewed by Lina Elise Grey.
ROPING LIONS IN THE GRAND CANYON
©1924 by Harper & Brothers; renewed 1951 by Lina Elise Grey.
STRANGE PARTNERS OF TWO-FOLD BAY
©1955 by American Weekly Magazine (Hearst Publishing Company);
renewed 1983 by Loren Grey and Betty Zane Grosso.
OF WHALES AND MEN
©1984 by Loren Grey.
THE TALE OF THE WILD MUSK OX
©1908 by Zane Grey; renewed 1936 by Zane Grey.

PUBLISHED BY SANTA BARBARA PRESS
1129 State St., Santa Barbara, California 93101
ISBN No. 0-915643-01-4
Library of Congress Catalog Card No. 84-50123

Designed and typeset in Garamond
by Jim Cook & Associates
Cover design by Alex Marshall
Pen-and-inks by Tom Huston

LIBRARY OF CONGRESS CATALOGING IN PUBLICATION DATA
GREY, ZANE, 1872-1939
The wolf tracker and other animal tales.
Contents: The wolf tracker—Roping lions in the Grand Canyon—
Strange partners of Two-Fold Bay—[etc.]
1. Animals—Fiction.   I. Grey, Loren.   II. Title.
PS3513.R6545A6   1984b   813'.52   84-50123
ISBN 0-915643-01-4 (pbk.)

CONTENTS

FOREWORD

THOSE WHO HAVE READ Zane Grey's western novels—and perhaps many others who may know him only by association—somehow seem to have identified him to the point of stereotype with cowboys, cattle rustling, gunmen, and fights with fierce Indians. However, few of his readers are aware of the fascination he had for the many aspects of nature. He gloried in the primitive wilderness: the dark, tangled rain forest, a waterless desert, an undammed river, or the sea in its infinite moods, placid and angry by turns. Though he wrote much more about the effects of nature on men and women who tried to make lives for themselves in a savage environment far from civilized amenities, he was just as captivated by the other inhabitants who lived with them in the wild, the animals who fought a similar battle to survive against an implacable nature which to him was somehow Darwinism and God inextricably combined in one. Many of these wild creatures he saw and depicted as having almost human characteristics, whether they were a band of fierce orcas who drove great whales into a lonely bay on the southeast coast of Australia so that the men in their little boats could go out and try to capture them; or a huge, gray wolf who for many years eluded all the efforts of a whole generation of men who tried to end his depredations against their livestock—until a strange, solitary tracker named Brink took up his trail. . . .

In this brand-new, high-quality anthology are a number of my father's very finest animal stories. The volume tells how they either served man or fought determinedly against him. Their exploits are recorded in as enthralling a fashion as the many novels that have earned him the reputation of one of the master storytellers of all time.

LOREN GREY
Woodland Hills, California
March 1984

THE WOLF TRACKER

INTRODUCTION

Bill Everett, a range hand, saw this wolf first. Telling about it, he called him an old gray Jasper. The name stuck, though now you seldom hear the Jasper tacked on. From that time on, stories began to drift into camp and town about the doings of Old Gray. He was a killer. The cowboys and hunters took to his trail with cow dogs and bear hounds. Though they routed him out of his lairs and chased him all over the mountains, they never caught him. Trappers camped all the way from the Cebique to Mt. Wilson, trying to trap him. They never heard of Old Gray touching a trap.

During the summer Old Gray lit out for the mountains and in the winter he took to the foothills of the ranges and I've heard cattlemen all over New Mexico say that he had killed $25,000 worth of stock—but that was years ago. It was impossible now to estimate the loss to ranchers. Old Gray played at the game. He'd run through a bunch of stock, hamstring a steer right and left until he was done with his fun. Then he'd pull down a yearling and eat what he wanted and travel on.

It seemed that no man could ever beat Old Gray, until a mysterious trapper by the name of Brink took up the trail....

ZANE GREY

THE WOLF TRACKER

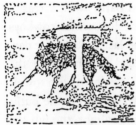HE HARD-RIDING cowmen of Adam's outfit returned to camp, that last day of the fall roundup, weary and brush-torn, begrimed with dust and sweat, and loud in their acclaims against Old Gray, the loafer wolf, notorious from the Cibeque across the black belt of rugged Arizona upland to Mount Wilson in New Mexico.

"Wal, reckon I allowed the Tonto had seen the last of Old Gray's big tracks," said Benson, the hawk-eyed foreman, as he slipped the bridle off his horse.

"An' for why?" queried Banty Smith, the little arguing rooster of the outfit. "Ain't Old Gray young yet—just in his prime? Didn't we find four carcasses of full-grown steers he'd pulled down last April over on Webber Creek? Shore he allus hit for high country in summer. What for did you think he'd not show up when the frost come?"

"Aw, Banty, cain't you savvy Ben?" drawled a long, lean rider. "He was jest voicin' his hopes."

"Yep, Ben is thet tender-hearted he'd weep over a locoed calf—if it happened to wear his brand," remarked Tim Bender, with a huge grin, as if he well knew he had acquitted himself wittily.

"Haw. Haw," laughed another rider. "Old Gray has shore made some deppredashuns on Ben's stock of twenty head. Most as much as one heifer."

"Wal, kid me all you like, boys," replied Benson, good-naturedly. "Reckon I had no call to think Old Gray wouldn't come back. He's done thet for years. But it's not onnatural to live in

13

hopes. An' it's hard luck we had to run acrost his tracks an' his work the last day of the roundup. Only last night the boss was sayin' he hadn't heard anythin' about Old Gray for months.

"Nobody heerd of anyone cashin' on thet five thousand dollars reward for Old Gray's scalp, either," replied Banty, with sarcasm.

Thus after the manner of the range the loquacious cowboys volleyed badinage while they performed the last tasks of the day.

Two streams met below the pine-shaded bench where the camp was situated; and some of the boys strode down with towels and soap to attend to ablutions that one washpan for the outfit made a matter of waiting. It was still clear daylight, though the sun had gone down behind a high timbered hill to the west. The blue haze that hung over the bench was not all campfire smoke. A rude log cabin stood above the fork of the streams, and near by the cook busied himself between his chuck wagon and the campfire. Both the cool, pine-scented air and the red gold patches of brush on the hillside told of the late October. The rich amber light of the woods had its reflection in the pools of the streams.

Adams, the boss of the outfit, had ridden over from his Tonto ranch at Spring Valley. He was a sturdy, well-preserved man of sixty, sharp of eye, bronze of face, with the stamp of self-made and prosperous rancher upon him.

"Ben, the boss is inquirin' aboot you," called Banty from the bench above the stream.

Whereupon the foreman clambered up the rocky slope, vigorously rubbing his ruddy face with a towel, and made his way to where Adams sat beside the campfire. In all respects, except regarding Old Gray, Benson's report was one he knew would be gratifying. This naturally he reserved until after Adams had expressed his satisfaction. Then he supplemented the news of the wolf.

"That loafer," ejaculated Adams, in dismay. "Why, only the other day I heard from my pardner, Barrett, an' he said the government hunters were trackin' Old Gray up Mount Wilson."

"Wal, boss thet may be true," responded the foreman. "But Old

Gray killed a yearlin' last night on the red ridge above Doubtful Canyon. I know his tracks like I do my hoss's. We found four kills today, an' I reckon all was the work of thet loafer. You don't need to see his tracks. He's shore a clean killer. An' sometimes he kills for the sake of killin'."

"I ain't sayin' I care about the money loss, though that old gray devil has cost me an' Barrett twenty-five hundred," replied Adams, thoughtfully. "But he's such a bloody murderer—the most aggravatin' varmint I ever—"

"Huh. Who's the gazabo comin' down the trail?" interrupted Benson, pointing up the bench.

"Stranger to me," said Adams. "Anybody know him?"

One by one the cowboys disclaimed knowledge of the unusual figure approaching. At that distance he appeared to be a rather old man, slightly bowed. But a second glance showed his shoulders to be broad and his stride the wonderful one of a mountaineer. He carried a pack on his back and a shiny carbine in his hand. His garb was ragged homespun, patched until it resembled a checkerboard.

"A stranger without a hoss," exclaimed Banty, as if that were an amazingly singular thing.

The man approached the campfire, and halted to lean the worn carbine against the woodpile. Then he unbuckled a strap round his breast and lifted a rather heavy pack from his back, to deposit it on the ground. It appeared to be a pack rolled in a rubber-lined blanket, out of which protruded the ends of worn snowshoes. When he stepped to the campfire he disclosed a strange physiognomy—the weather-beaten face of a matured man of the open, mapped by deep lines, strong, hard, a rugged mask, lighted by penetrating, quiet eyes of gray.

"Howdy, stranger. Get down an' come in," welcomed Adams, with the quaint, hearty greeting always resorted to by a Westerner.

"How do. I reckon I will," replied the man, extending big brown hands to the fire. "Are you Adams, the cattleman?"

"You've got me. But I can't just place you, stranger."

"Reckon not. I'm new in these parts. My name's Brink. I'm a tracker."

"Glad to meet you, Brink," replied Adams, curiously. "These are some of my boys. Set down an' rest. I reckon you're tired an' hungry. We'll have grub soon. . . . Tracker, you said? Now, I just don't savvy what you mean."

"I've been prospector, trapper, hunter, most everythin'," replied Brink as he took the seat offered. "But I reckon my callin' is to find tracks. Tracker of men, hosses, cattle, wild animals— 'specially sheep-killen' silvertips an' stock-killen' wolves."

"Aha. You don't say?" ejaculated Adams, suddenly shifting from genial curiosity to keen interest. "An' you're after that five thousand dollars we cattlemen offered for Old Gray's scalp?"

"Nope. I hadn't thought of the reward. I heard of it, up in Colorado, same time I heard of this wolf that's run amuck so long on these ranges. An' I've come down here to kill him."

Adams showed astonishment along with his interest, but his silence and expression did not approach the incredulity manifested by the men of his outfit. Banty winked a roguish eye at his comrades; Benson leaned forward with staring eyes and dropping jaw; Tim Bender made covert and significant signs to indicate the stranger had wheels in his head; the other riders were amiably nonplussed as to the man's sanity. Nothing more than the response of these men was needed to establish the reputation of Old Gray, the loafer wolf. But Brink did not see these indications; he was peering into the fire.

"So—ho. You have?" exclaimed Adams, breaking the silence. "Wal, now, Brink, that's good of you. We sure appreciate your intent. Would you mind tellin' us how you mean to set about killin' Old Gray?"

"Reckon I told you I was a tracker," rejoined Brink, curtly.

"Hell, man. We've had every pack of hounds in two states on the track of that wolf."

"Is he on the range now?" queried Brink, totally ignoring Adams's strong protestation.

Adams motioned to his foreman to reply to this question. Benson made evident effort to be serious.

"I seen his tracks less'n two hours ago. He killed a yearlin' last night."

At these words Brink turned his gaze from the fire to the speaker. What a remarkable fleeting flash crossed his rugged face. It seemed one of passion. It passed, and only a gleam of eye attested to strange emotion under that seamed and lined mask of bronze. His gaze returned to the fire, and the big hands, that he held palms open to the heat, now clasped each other, in strong and tense action. Only Adams took the man seriously, and his attitude restrained the merriment his riders certainly felt.

"Adams, would you mind tellin' me all you know about this wolf?" asked the stranger, presently.

"Say, man," expostulated Adams, still with good nature, "it wouldn't be polite to keep you from eatin' an' sleepin'. We don't treat strangers that way in this country."

"Old Gray has a history, then?" inquired Brink, as intent as if he had been concerned with the case of a human being.

"Humph. Reckon I couldn't tell you all about him in a week," said the cattleman, emphatically.

"It wouldn't matter to me how long you'd take," returned Brink, thoughtfully.

At that Adams laughed outright. This queer individual had not in the least considered waste of time to a busy rancher. Manifestly he thought only of the notorious wolf. Adams eyed the man a long speculative moment, divided between amusement and doubt. Brink interested him. Having had to deal with many and various kinds of men, Adams was not quite prepared to take this stranger as the young riders took him. Adams showed the shrewdness of appreciation of the many-sidedness of human nature. Brink's face and garb and pack were all extraordinarily different from what was usually met with on these ranges. He had arrived on foot, but he was not a tramp. Adams took keener note of the quiet face, the deep chest, the muscular hands, the wiry body, and the powerful legs. No cowboy, for all his riding, ever had wonderful legs like these. The man was a walker.

These deductions, slight and unconvincing as they were, united with an amiability that was characteristic of Adams, persuaded him to satisfy the man's desire to hear about the wolf.

"All right, Brink, I'll tell you somethin' of Old Gray—at leastways till the cook calls us to come an' get it. . . . There used to be a good many loafers—timber wolves, we called them—in this country. But they're gettin' scarce. Accordin' to the hunters there's a small bunch of loafers rangin' from Black Butte to Clear Creek Canyon. That's a deer country, an' we cattlemen don't run much stock over there. Now an' then a cowboy will see a wolf track, or hear one bay. But outside of Old Gray we haven't had much loss from loafers of late years.

"Naturally there are lots of stories in circulation about this particular wolf. Some of them are true. I can't vouch for his parentage, or whether he has mixed blood. Seven or eight, maybe ten years ago, some trapper lost a husky—one of them regular Alaskan snow-sled dogs—over in the Mazatzels. Never found him. Some natives here claim Old Gray is a son of this husky, his mother bein' one of the range loafers. Another story is about a wolf escapin' from a circus over heah in a railroad wreck years ago. I remember well the report told at Winslow. A young gray wolf got away. This escaped wolf might be Old Gray. No one can ever tell that. But both stories are interestin' enough to think about.

"The name Old Gray doesn't seem to fit this particular wolf, because it's misleadin'. He's gray, yes, almost white, but he's not old. Bill Everett, a range hand, saw this wolf first. Tellin' about it he called him an old gray Jasper. The name stuck, though now you seldom hear the Jasper tacked on.

"From that time stories began to drift into camp an' town about the doin's of Old Gray. He was a killer. Cowboys an' hunters took to his trail with cow dogs an' bear hounds. But though they routed him out of his lairs an' chased him all over, they never caught him. Trappers camped all the way from the Cibeque to Mount Wilson, tryin' to trap him. I never heard of Old Gray touchin' a trap.

"In summer Old Gray lit out for the mountains. In winter he took to the foothills an' ranges. I've heard cattlemen over in New Mexico say he had killed twenty-five thousand dollars' worth of stock. But that was years ago. It would be impossible now to estimate the loss to ranchers. Old Gray played at the game. He'd run through a bunch of stock, hamstringin' right an' left, until he had enough of his fun, then he'd pull down a yearlin', eat what he wanted, an' travel on.

"He didn't always work alone. Sometimes he'd have several loafers with him. Two years ago I saw his tracks with at least four other wolves. That was on my pardner's ranch at Vermajo Park, New Mexico. But Old Gray always was an' is a lone wolf. He didn't trust company. Accordin' to report he'd led off more than one she dog, always shepherds. They never came back. It's a good bet he led them away, for his tracks were seen, an' perhaps he killed them.

"The government hunters have been tryin' to get him, these several years. They don't tell about this hunt any more. But the forest rangers sometimes make fun at the expense of these predatory game hunters of the government. Anyway, so far as I know, Old Gray has never been scratched. My personal opinion is this. He's a magnificent wild brute, smarter than any dog. An' you know how intelligent dogs can be. Well, Old Gray is too savage, too wild, too keen to be caught by the ordinary means employed so far. . . . There, Brink, is the plain blunt facts from a blunt man. If you listened to a lot of the gossip about Old Gray you'd be sure locoed."

"Much obliged," replied Brink, with a break in his rapt intensity. "Have you ever seen this loafer?"

"No, I never had the good luck," replied Adams. "Nor have many men. But Benson, here, has seen him."

"What's he look like?" queried Brink, turning eagerly to the foreman.

"Wal, Old Gray is about the purtiest wild varmint I ever clapped my eyes on," drawled Benson, slow and cool, as if to tantalize this wolf hunter. "He's big—a heap bigger'n any loafer I ever saw before—an' he's gray all right, a light gray, with a black ring part round his neck, almost like a ruff. He's a bold cus, too. He stood watchin' me, knowin' darn well he was out of gunshot."

"Now what kind of a track does he make?"

"Wal, jest a wolf track bigger's you ever seen before. Almost as big as a hoss track. When you see it once, you'll never forget."

"Where did you run across that track last?"

Benson squatted down before the fire, and with his hand smoothed a flat clear place in the dust, on which he began to trace lines.

"Heah, foller up this creek till you come to a high falls. Climb up the slope on the right. You'll head out on a cedar an' pinon ridge. It's red dirt, most all soft. Halfway up this ridge from there you'll strike a trail. It runs this heah way. Foller it round under the bluff till you strike Old Gray's tracks. I seen them this mawnin', fresh as could be. Sharp an' clean in the dust. He was makin' for the Rim, I reckon soon after he had killed the heifer."

By this time all the cowboys were grouped round the central figures. Banty appeared to be the only one not seriously impressed. As to the others, something about Brink and the way he had moved Adams to talk, had inhibited for the moment their characteristic humor.

Brink slowly rose from his scrutiny of the map that Benson had drawn in the dust. His penetrating gaze fixed on Adams.

"I'll kill your old gray wolf," he said.

His tone, his manner, seemed infinitely more than his simple words. They all combined to make an effect that seemed indefinable, except in the case of Banty, who grew red in the face. Manifestly Banty took this man's statement as astounding and ridiculous. The little cowboy enjoyed considerable reputation as a hunter—a reputation that he cherished, and which, to his humiliation, had not been lived up to by his several futile hunts after Old Gray.

"Aw, now—so you'll kill thet loafer," he ejaculated, in the most elaborate satire possible for a cowboy. "Wal, Mr. Brink, would you mind tellin' us jest when you'll perpetuate this execushun? Shore all the outfits in the Tonto will want to see Old Gray's scalp. We'll give a dance to celebrate. . . . Say when you'll fetch his skin down—tomorrow around sunup, or mebbe next day, seein' you have to travel on shank's mare—or possible the day after."

Banty's drawling scorn might never have been spoken, for all the intended effect it had on the wolf hunter. Brink was beyond the levity of a cowboy.

"Reckon I can't say just when I'll kill Old Gray," he replied, with something sonorous in his voice. "It might be any day, accordin' to luck. But if he's the wolf you all say he is, it'll take long."

"You don't say," spoke up Banty. "Wal, by gosh, my walkin' gent, I figgered you had some Injun medicine that you could put on Old Gray's tail."

The cowboy's roared. Adams showed constraint in his broad grin. Brink suffered no offense, no sign of appreciating the ridicule. Thoughtfully he bent again to the fire, and did not hear the cook's lusty call to supper.

"Never mind the boys," said Adams, kindly, putting a hand on the bowed shoulder. "Come an' eat with us."

II

THE MORNING SUN had not yet melted the hoarfrost from the brush when Brink halted in the trail before huge wolf tracks in the red dust.

"Same as any wolf tracks, only big," he soliloquized. "Biggest I ever saw—even in Alaska."

Whereupon he leaned his shiny carbine against a pine sapling, and lifted his pack from his shoulders, all the time with gaze riveted on the trail. Then, with head bent, he walked slowly along until he came to a place where all four tracks of the wolf showed plainly. Here he got to his knees, scrutinizing the imprints, photographing them on his inward eye, taking intent and grave stock of them, as if these preliminaries in the stalking of a wolf were a ritual. For moments he remained motionless, like one transfixed. Presently he relaxed, and seating himself beside the trail, seemed to revel in a strange, tranquil joy.

Brink's state of mind was a composite of a lifetime's feelings, thoughts, actions, never comprehensible to him. As a boy of three he had captured his first wild creature—a squirrel that he tamed and loved, and at last freed. All his early boyhood he had been a haunter of the woods and hills, driven to the silent places and the abode of the wild. At sixteen he had run away from school and home; at fifty he knew the west from the cold borders of the Yukon to the desert-walled Yaqui. Through those many and eventful years the occupations of men had held him, but never for long. Caravans, mining camps, freighting posts, towns and settlements, ranches and camps had known him, though never for any length of time. Women had never drawn him, much less men.

Again the solitude and loneliness of the wilderness claimed him; and his eyes feasted on the tracks of a beast commonly supposed to be stronger, keener than any human. Around these two facts clung the fibers of the spell that possessed Brink's soul.

The October morning seemed purple in the shade, golden in the sun. A profound and unbroken stillness held this vast cedar slope in thrall. A spicy tang, cold to the nostrils, permeated the air. The sheath-barked cedars and the junipers with their lavender-hued berries stretched a patchwork of light and shadow across the trail. Far down, the ridged sweep of timbered country fell. Beyond the black vague depths of the Basin rose the sharp, ragged mountains to the south. Above him towered bold promontories of rock, fringed by green, clearly etched against the blue. Nothing of mankind tainted this loneliness for Brink—nothing save the old, seldom-trodden trail, and that bore the tracks of an enormous wolf, wildest of all American animals.

Brink's serenity had returned—the familiar state that had ceased at the end of his last pursuit. This huge track was a challenge. But this strange egotism did not appear to be directed toward the hunters and cowboys who had failed on Old Gray's trail. Rather toward the wolf. The issue was between him and the great loafer. Here began the stalk that for Brink had but one conclusion. The wonderful tracks showed sharply in the dust. Old Gray had passed along there yesterday. He was somewhere up or down those ragged slopes. Cunning as he was, he had to hold contact with earth and rock. He had to slay and eat. He must leave traces of his nature, his life, his habit, and his action. To these Brink would address himself, with all the sagacity of an old hunter, but with something infinitely more—a passion which he did not understand.

"Wal, Old Gray, I'm on your track," muttered Brink, grimly; and strapping the heavy pack on his broad shoulders, he took up the carbine and strode along the trail.

It pleased Brink to find that his first surmise was as correct as if he had cognizance of Old Gray's instincts. The wolf tracks soon sheered off the trail. Old Gray was not now a hunting or a prowling wolf. He was a traveling wolf, but he did not keep to the easygoing, direct trail.

On soft ground like this, bare except for patches of brush and brown mats under the cedar and pinon trees, Brink could discern the wolf tracks far ahead. Old Gray was light-footed, but he had weight, and his trail along here was as easy for the keen eyes of the tracker as if he had been traveling on wet ground or snow. Where he did not leave tracks there was a pressed tuft of grass or a disturbed leaf or broken twig or dislodged bit of stone, or an unnatural displacement of the needles under the pinons.

The trail led down over the uneven ridges and gullies of the

slope, down into timbered thickets, and on through an increas-
ingly rugged and wild country, to the dark shade of a deep gorge,
where the melodious murmur of a stream mingled with the
mourn of a rising wind in the lofty pines and spruces. The wolf
had drunk his fill, leaving two huge tracks in the wet sand along
the brookside. Brink could not find tracks on gravel and boulders,
so he crossed the wide bottom of the gorge, and after a while
found Old Gray's trail on the opposite slope. Before he struck it
he had believed the wolf was heading for high country.

Brink tracked him over a forested ridge and down into an
intersecting canyon, where on the rocks of a dry stream bed the
trail failed. This did not occasion the wolf tracker any concern.
Old Gray would most likely choose that rugged lonely stream bed
and follow it to where the canyon headed out above. Brink, in
such cases as this, trusted to his instincts. Many times he had been
wrong, but more often he had been right. To this end he slowly
toiled up the rough ascent, halting now and then to rest a
moment, eyes roving from side to side. It was a steep ascent, and
grew rougher, narrower, and more shaded as he climbed. At
length he came to pools of water in rocky recesses, where the
sand and gravel bars showed the tracks of cattle, bear, and deer.
But if Old Gray had passed on up that narrowing canyon he had
avoided the water holes.

Patches of maple and thickets of oak covered the steep slopes,
leading up to the base of cracked and seamed cliffs, and they in
turn sheered up to where the level rim shone black-fringed
against the blue. Here the stream bed was covered with the red
and gold and purple of fallen autumn leaves. High up the thickets
had begun to look shaggy. The sun, now at the zenith, fell hot
upon Brink's head. He labored on to climb out a narrow defile
that led to the level forest above.

Here the wind blew cool. Brink rested a moment, gazing down
into the colorful void, and across the black rolling leagues to the
mountains. Then he strode east along the precipice, very carefully

searching for the wolf trail he had set out upon. In a mile of slow travel he did not discover a sign of Old Gray. Retracing his steps, he traveled west for a like distance, without success. Whereupon he returned to the head of the canyon out of which he had climbed, and there, divesting himself of his pack, he set about a more elaborate scrutiny of ground, grass, moss, and rock. He searched from the rim down into an aspen swale that deepened into a canyon, heading away from the rim. He had no reason to believe Old Gray would travel this way, except that long experience had taught him where to search first for tracks. And quite abruptly he came upon the huge footprints of the loafer, made in soft black mud beside elk tracks that led into a hole where water had recently stood.

"Hah," ejaculated Brink. "You're interested in that yearlin' elk. . . . Wal, Old Gray, I'll let this do for today."

Brink returned to get his pack, and carried it down into the ravine, to a point where he found clear water. Here he left the pack in the fork of a tree, and climbed out to the level forest, to hunt for meat.

The afternoon was far spent and the warmth of the westering sun soon declined. Brink found deer and wild turkey signs in abundance, and inside of the hour he had shot a two-year-old spike-horn buck. He cut out the haunches and packed them back to where he had decided to camp.

With a short-handled ax he carried in his belt he trimmed off the lower branches of a thick-foliaged spruce and, cutting them into small pieces, he laid them crosswise to serve as a bed. Then he unrolled his pack. The snowshoes he hung on the stub of a branch; the heavy, rubber-covered blanket he spread on the spruce boughs, and folded it so that the woolen side would be under him and over him while he slept. Next he started a large fire of dead sticks.

Brink's pack of supplies weighed about fifty pounds. He had three sheet-iron utensils, which telescoped together, a tin cup, a spoon, matches, towel, and soap. His food was carried in canvas sacks of varying sizes, all tightly tied. He had coffee, sugar, salt, and the sugar sack was almost disproportionately large. No flour, no butter, no canned milk. The biggest sack contained pemmican, a composite food of small bulk and great nourishing power. The chief ingredients were meat and nuts. This prepared food Brink had learned to rely upon during long marches in Alaska. His next largest sack contained dried apples. By utilizing, when possible, the game meat of the forest Brink expected this supply to last a long time, possibly until he had run down the wolf.

Like those of an Indian on the march, Brink's needs were few. He prepared his frugal meal, ate it with the relish and gratefulness of a man used to the wilderness. Then before darkness overtook him he cut the fresh deer meat into strips so that it would dry readily.

Twilight found his tasks ended for the day. The melancholy autumn night darkened and stole down upon him, cold and sharp, with threads of cloud across the starry sky. The wind moaned in the black pines above, and seemed to warn of the end of autumn. There was no other sound except the sputter of the campfire.

Brink's enjoyment lay in spreading his horny palms to the genial heat of the red coals. His attitude was one of repose and serenity. If there was sadness about his lonely figure, it was something of which he had no conscious thought. Brink had only dim remembrance of home and family, vague things far back in the past. He had never loved a woman. He had lived apart from men, aloof even when the accident of life and travel had thrown him into camps or settlements. Once he had loved a dog. Seldom did his mind dwell on the past, and then only in relation to some pursuit or knowledge that came to him from the contiguity of the present task.

He liked the loneliness, the wildness, the solitude. He seemed to be part of them. When a very young boy he had been forced by a stepmother to hate a house. As a child he had been punished at the table, and never in his life afterward could he outgrow hate of a dining room and the fear that had been instilled into his consciousness.

Night settled down black, with but few stars showing through the gathering clouds. Listening and watching and feeling were sensorial habits with Brink. Rain or snow breathed on the chill wind. He hailed the possibility of either with satisfaction. It was through the snow that he meant to track Old Gray to his last lair. When the heat of the fire died out Brink went to his bed, rolled in the blanket, and at once fell asleep.

The cold, raw dawn found him stirring. A blanket of cloud had prevented a white frost on the grass, but there glistened a film of ice on the brook. As the sun came up it brightened a blue sky, mostly clear. The drift of the thin clouds was from the southwest, and they were traveling fast.

Before the sun had warmed out the shade of the canyon, Brink, with pack on his back and rifle in hand, had taken up Old Gray's trail. It was easy to follow. The wolf showed a preference for the open canyon, and in many places left plain imprints in the sand. The canyon, running away from the rim, deepened and widened; and its disconnected pools of water at last became a running stream. Elk and deer and turkeys filed before Brink; likewise scattered bands of cattle and an occasional bunch of wild horses.

Evidently the great wolf was not losing time to place distance between him and his last kill. Brink found no more sign of his evincing interest in any tracks. About noon, by which time Brink had trailed the animal fully ten miles down the canyon, seldom losing the tracks for long, Old Gray took to an intersecting canyon, rough-walled and brushy, and soon he went up into the rocks. It took Brink all afternoon to find where the wolf had lain, but Brink would gladly have spent days for such a triumph.

"Aha, you old gray devil," he soliloquized, as he bent his gaze on a snug retreat under shelving rocks, where showed the betraying impress of feet and body of the wolf. "So you have to sleep an' rest, huh? Wal, I reckon you can't get along without killin' an' eatin' too. Old Gray, you're bound to leave tracks, an' I'll find them."

Brink camped that night under the cliff where Old Gray had slept the day before. Next day he spent much time finding tracks along the water course in this narrow canyon, and succeeding ones that led off to the west. This canyon soon opened out into grassy ovals that appeared to be parks for elks. Brink surprised a herd of eleven, two bulls with enormous spread of antlers, a young bull, several cow elks, and four calves. They trooped up the canyon, trampling the trails and sandy spots. Brink kept on, feeling sure that he had the general direction Old Gray had adopted. This held to the west and slightly northward, which course led toward the wildest country in that section, deep canyon, rough buttes, and matted jungles of pine saplings. Here, according to information Brink had obtained from the cowboys, ranged the last of the timber wolves known to exist in Arizona. It was Brink's conviction that Old Gray knew the country well.

The band of elks soon climbed out of the canyon. Beyond that point the bare spots showed only old tracks of game. At length Brink came to a beaver dam; and on the very edge of it, deep in the wet mud, showed the unmistakable tracks of the giant wolf. Brink had another of those strange thrills, an inward leaping of blood, somehow savage. From that point Old Gray's tracks showed in the wet places up and down the banks of the narrow ponds of water. He had been vastly curious about these dams and mounds erected by the beaver. Everywhere he left tracks. But Brink could not find any sign of the wolf's catching a beaver unawares. The beaver of this colony had been at work that night cutting the aspen trees and dragging boughs and sections of trunks under the water.

Sunset came before Brink had found a track of the wolf leading away from that park. Still, he made camp satisfied with the day. Any day in which he found a single fresh track of this wolf was indeed time well spent. Unless he were extremely lucky, he must lose the trail for days. His hope was that he might keep the general direction Old Gray had taken until the snow began to fall. So far his hope had been more than fulfilled.

The night was clearer and colder than the preceding ones, yet there were thin, ragged clouds sweeping up out of the southwest, and a moaning wind that whined of storm. Late October without rain or snow was most unusual for that latitude. Brink camped near the beaver dam, and the cold windy darkness found him snug in his blanket. During the night he was awakened by a yelp of coyotes, and later by a pattering of sleet on the dry brush. A black cloud was scudding across the sky. It passed with the threatening storm. Morning broke brighter than ever. He began to fear wet weather had been sidetracked indefinitely. But after all there was no good in his being impatient. If he lost Old Gray's trail on dry ground, sooner or later he would find it again. This three-hundred-mile strip of comparatively low country was the winter range of the great wolf. He had a taste for young cattle. It was unlikely that he would go back into the high altitude of his summer range in the New Mexico mountains.

Brink's good luck persisted. He discovered Old Gray's tracks leading up out of the canyon. The direction then was all he could hope for at present, because, naturally, he expected to lose the trail on the hard and dry ridge tops. He did lose it. All signs of the wolf vanished. But Brink had ascertained that Old Gray had traveled almost straight toward the rough country to the north-west. Therefore Brink zig-zagged the ridges and canyons for three days without a sign of his quarry's movements. He wondered if the wolf had made a kill during this period. He traveled into a cut-up country of deep canyons and rock ridges, overgrown with heavy forest. He saw no more elk or bear signs, but deer tracks became as plentiful as cattle tracks in a corral.

Late on the afternoon of that third day, as Brink was hunting for a suitable camp, he came to an open glade in the pine forest.

In the center of it was a pond of surface water about an acre in size. Deer tracks both old and fresh were numerous. Brink, after deciding the water was safe to drink, deposited his pack in a likely camp spot amid a thicket of pine saplings, and started to walk round the pond. Before he had gone halfway he encountered wolf tracks, made the night before. They were loafer marks, but not Old Gray's.

"Wal, wolf tracks cross each other on any range," decided Brink. "Reckon I'll take to these. . . . Ahuh. There's been a couple of loafers here, an' one of them has a bad foot. Been in a trap, mebbe."

Brink made camp leisurely. He was getting into wolf country. The sunset shone ominously overcast and threatening. The temperature had moderated and the feeling of frost gave way to dampness. Brink cleared a space in the pine thicket, and erected a shelving lean-to on the windward side. Under this he made his bed. His next move was to gather a goodly store of dry firewood and to pile it under the shelter. After that he cooked his meal, and this time, to his satisfaction, he broiled a young turkey he had shot the day before.

Night settled down like a black blanket, starless and gloomy. The wind moaned louder than usual. Brink soliloquized that the wind was warning Old Gray to leave the country before the fatal snow fell. Brink enjoyed this meal more than any heretofore on this hunt. The wild scene, the somber tarn, the menacing solitude were all to his liking. He was settling into his routine. Contrary to his custom on the preceding nights, he sat up a long time, and whether he had his face to the fire or his back, his palms were always spread to the comforting heat. Brink looked and listened with more than usual attention during this vigil beside the campfire. It appeared that the wind grew more raw, damper.

"Rain or snow sure," he muttered, and the note boded ill to certain wild denizens of that forestland.

At length drowsiness made his eyelids heavy and he sought his bed under the shelter of pine boughs. Sleep claimed him. He awakened with a feeling that only a moment had elapsed, but he could tell by the dead campfire how misleading this was. Something had roused him.

Suddenly from the dark forest on the cold wind came the deep, wild bay of a hunting wolf. With a start Brink sat up. A quiver ran over him. How intensely he listened. No other wild sound in nature had such power over him. It seemed as if this bay came from a vague dim past. Again it peeled out, but with a sharper note, not greatly different from that of a hunting hound.

"Loafers trailin' a deer," said Brink. "Two of them, mebbe more."

Again he heard the bays, growing farther away, and another time, quite indistinct. After that the weird moaning solitude of the forest remained undisturbed.

Brink lay back in his blanket, but not to sleep. He would lie awake now for a long while. How that wolf bay brought back memories of the frozen northland. All wolves were of the same species. They loved hot blood. It was their savage instinct to feed ravenously off a still-living victim.

Brink imagined he heard deep low bays back in the forest. Always the wind made the sound for which the eager ears were attuned. And even when he was not listening for any particular sound, the wind deceived with its wild cry of beast, its wail of lost humans, its mourning for the dead, its distant approach to a trampling army.

All the same, Brink again suddenly sat up. "Say, have I got a nightmare?" He turned his ear away from the cold wind, and holding his breath, he listened. Did he hear a bay or a moan in the forest? Long he remained stiff, intent.

The wolves had resorted to a trick Brink knew well. The pack had split into several parts, one of which relayed the deer for a time, driving it round while the others rested. In Brink's experience the trick was common for a pack that had a great leader.

Once again in the succeeding hour Old Gray passed near

Brink's camp, ringing out that hoarse cry of hunger for blood.
Long after the sound had rolled through the forest, to die away it
lingered on his ears. But it did not come again.

Instead, something happened to Brink which sent a tight cold
prickle to his skin. It was the touch of soft misty snow on his face.
A tiny seeping rustle, almost indistinguishable, fell about him on
the brush. Snow. Cloud and wind and atmosphere had combined
in the interest of the wolftracker.

                                  III

A LOWERING GRAY DAWN disclosed the forest mantled in a wet
snow, deep enough to cover the ground and burden the trees. The
wind had eased somewhat and was colder, which facts augured for
clearing weather. Thin broken clouds moved close to the tops of
the loftiest pines.

"Wal, reckon it's only a skift," remarked Brink, as his gaze
swept the white-carpeted glade, with its round pond of dark
water in the center. "But it's snow, an' right here my trackin'
begins. If it melts, it'll leave the ground soft. If it doesn't, well an'
good."

Brink was singularly happy. The raw dawn with its changed
forest-world would have alienated most men, but he was not that
kind of a hunter. The Indian summer days were past. The white
banner of winter had been unrolled. Moreover, Old Gray had
passed in the night, ringing his wild and unearthly voice down
the aisles of the forest. Somehow Brink had no doubt that the
hoarse hound-like bay belonged to the wolf he was stalking.

"I know his tracks," said Brink, "an' I've heard him yelp.
Sooner or later I'll see him. Wal now, that'll be a sight.... But I
reckon I'm over reachin' this good luck."

A pale light behind the gray clouds in the east marked the rise
of the sun. Only a few inches of snow had fallen. As Brink trudged

away from his camp, out into the white glade, he was victim to an eagerness and joy extraordinary in a man. But the most driving instinct of his life had been the hunting of animals by the tracks they left. As a boy it had been play; in manhood it had become a means of livelihood; now it was a passion. Therefore he hailed the pure white covering of snow with pleasure and affection.

His educated eyes sought the ground. Here were the tiny footprints of a chipmunk; next the ragged tracks of a squirrel, showing where his tail had dragged; coyote and fox had also visited the pond since the fall of snow. Brink crossed the open glade to enter the forest. A blue jay screeched at him from an oak tree and a red squirrel chattered angrily. Brink passed under a spruce where the little squirrel had already dug for the seed cones he had stored for winter food.

Brink espied the wolf and buck tracks fully fifty yards ahead of him. Soon he stood over them. The tracks had been made before the snow had ceased to fall, yet they were clear enough to be read by the hunter. The buck had been running. Two wolves had been chasing him, but neither was Old Gray. After a long scrutiny of the tracks Brink left them and stalked on deeper into the forest. He crossed the trail of a lynx. What a betrayer of wild beasts was the white snow they loved so well. Brink seemed to read the very thoughts of that prowling hunting cat.

Toward noon the sun came out, lighting up the forest, until it appeared to be an enchanted place of gleaming aisles, of brown-barked trunks and white-burdened branches. Everywhere snow was sliding, slipping, falling from the trees. Rainbows showed through the mist. The aspens with their golden leaves and the oaks with their bronze belied the wintry forest scene. On the snow lay leaves of yellow and red and brown, fallen since the storm. Pine needles were floating down from the lofty pines, and aspen leaves, like butterflies, fluttered in the air. Through the green-and-white canopy overhead showed rifts in the clouds and sky of deep blue. Though the forest was white and cold, autumn yielded reluctantly to winter, squirrels and jays and woodpeckers acclaimed a welcome to the sun.

Brink missed none of the beauty, though his grim task absorbed him. All of the moods of nature were seriously accepted by him. He was a man of the open.

He arrived at last where the buck had reached the end of his tragic race, and by some strange paradox of nature the woodland scene was one of marvelous color and beauty. Over a low swale the pine monarchs towered and the silver spruces sent their exquisite spiral crests aloft. On one side a sheltered aspen thicket still clung tenaciously to its golden fluttering foliage. Maples burned in cerise and magenta and scarlet hues.

Underfoot, however, the beauty of this spot had been marred. Here the buck had been overtaken, pulled down, torn to pieces, and devoured, even to the cracking of its bones. The antlers, the skull, part of the ragged hide were left, ghastly evidences of the ferocity of that carnage. The snow had been crushed, dragged, wiped, and tracked out, yet there were left vestiges soaked by blood. Coyotes had visited the scene, and these scavengers had quarreled over the bones.

As Brink had seen the beauty of the colorful forest, so now he viewed the record of the tragic balance of nature. The one to him was the same as the other. He did not hate Old Gray for being the leader in this butchery of a gentle forest creature.

"Wal now, I wonder how long he'll trail with this pack of loafers," he soliloquized. "If I was guessin' I'd say not long."

How different from those running wolf tracks he had been following were these leisurely trotting paces that led up to the rough bluffs. Brink calculated they had been made just before dawn. The wolves had gorged. They were heavy and sluggish. At this moment they would be sleeping off that orgy of blood and meat. Brink reached the foot of a very rugged butte, not so high as the adjoining one, Black Butte, which dominated the landscape, but of a nature which rendered it almost insurmountable for man.

Manzanita and live oak choked all the interstices between the rugged broken fragments of cliff. Obstacles, however, never daunted Brink.

Brink strode on, keen to find the second trail of wolves, and to settle absolutely the question as to Old Gray's presence with this marauding band of loafers. There might be two great-voiced wolves on the range. But the track would decide. When at length he encountered the trail he was seeking, abruptly at the top of a low ridge, he stood motionless, gazing with rapt, hard eyes. Two loafers besides Old Gray had chased the buck along here. So there were at least five in the pack.

"I was right," said Brink, with a deep breath. Old Gray's tracks in the snow were identical with those he left in the dust. Yet how vastly more potent to Brink. For snow was the medium by which he had doomed the great timber wolf. Without snow to betray him Old Gray would have been as safe as the eagles in their trackless air. This, then, was the moment of exceeding significance to Brink. Here again the test of endurance. All the hunters who had failed on Old Gray's trail had matched their intelligence with his cunning instinct. The hounds that had chased the wolf had failed because the fleet and powerful animal had outdistanced them and run out of the country. But Brink did not work like other hunters. His idea was the result of long stalking of wild game. And this moment when he gazed down into the huge tracks in the snow was one in which he felt all the tremendous advantage in his favor. Somewhere in a rocky recess or cave Old Gray was now sleeping after the chase and the gorge, unaware of his relentless and inevitable human foe. But Brink was in possession of facts beyond the ken of any wild creature. Perhaps his passion was to prove the superiority of man over beast.

Without a word he set off on the trail so plain in the snow, and as he stalked along he sought to read through those telltale tracks the speed and strength of the buck, the cunning and endurance of the wolves, and all the wild nature suggested therein. Through

level open forest, down ridge and over swale, into thickets of
maple and aspen, across parks where bleached grass glistened out
of the snow, he strode on with the swing of a mountaineer. He
did not tire. His interest had mounted until the hours seemed
moments.

Cougar tracks, deer tracks, turkey tracks crossed the trail he
was following. It swung in a ragged circle, keeping clear of rocks,
canyons, and the windfalls where running would be difficult.
Brink passed three relay stations where resting and running
wolves had met; and at the last of these all five wolves took the
trail of the doomed buck. They had chased him all night. Their
baying had kept all of them within hearing of each other. The
resting relay had cunningly cut in or across at times, thus to drive
the buck out of a straightaway race.

Laying aside pack and snowshoes, with rifle in hand he essayed
the ascent. Part of the time over rock and the rest through the
brush he made his way, wholly abandoning the direction of the
wolf trail.

After an hour of prodigious labor Brink reached the base of a
low bulging wall of rock, marked by cracks and fissures. The snow
was somewhat deeper at this altitude and afforded a perfect
medium in which to track animals. Bobcat, lynx, their lairs. And
then, around on the windward cougar, fox, and coyote had
climbed the bluff. There Brink found the trail of the loafers. The
difference between their sagacity and that of the other wild beasts
was indicated by their selection of the windy side of the bluff.
Brink tracked them toward the dark hole of a den. Upon reaching
the aperture he was not in the least surprised to see Old Gray's
tracks leading out. The other loafers were still in the cave. But Old
Gray had gotten a scent on the wind, perhaps even in his sleep,
and he had departed alone.

"Wal, you bloody loafers can sleep, for all we care," soliloquized
Brink. "Old Gray an' me have work."

Somehow Brink took exceeding pleasure in the fact that the

great wolf had been too cunning to be holed up by a hunter. This was just what Brink had anticipated. Old Gray was beginning to show the earmarks of a worthy antagonist. Brink thought he was going to have respect and admiration for the loafer.

Brink knelt to study the tracks, and did not soon come to a conclusion.

"Reckon he scented me," he said finally. "But I wonder if he suspects he's bein' tracked.... Wal now, when he learns that."

The wolf tracker clambered around over the slabs of rock and under the cliffs until he found where Old Gray had started to descend the bluff. Then Brink retraced his steps, finding the return as easy as the climb had been hard. Once more donning his pack, he set out, keeping to the forest where it edged on the rising ground. Before he had gone a mile he encountered Old Gray's big tracks.

Here Brink sustained a genuine surprise. He had made sure the wolf would head straight for the northwest, instinctively making for the wildest country. But instead the tracks struck into the woods straight as a beeline, and no more were they leisurely.

"Huh. The son-of-a-gun. If he circles I'll sure take off my hat to him," said Brink.

With his mountaineer's stride Brink set off through open forest, downhill, over a few inches of snow, making four miles an hour. Brink did not circle. Vastly curious did the hunter become. It looked as if the wolf was making a shortcut for somewhere. If he kept up this course he would soon cross his back trail. Perhaps that was just what Old Gray had in mind. Still, if he suspected he was being pursued, why had he not circled long ago to find what was following his tracks? Brink reflected that there was no absolute telling what a wild animal might do. He had trailed grizzly bears in the snow, and found they had abruptly turned uphill a little way, then had gone back, closer and closer to the lower trail, at last to lie and wait for him in ambush.

A wolf, especially a great loafer like Old Gray, rather enjoyed

such a short chase as men and dogs gave him. He could run right
away from them. His chief resource was his speed. But Old Gray
had not heard the bay of hounds or yell of men or crack of
iron-shod hoof on stone. He was very probably suspicious that
something new hung in the wind.

Brink warmed to the pursuit, both physically and in his spirit.
By and by the thing would narrow down to the supreme test
between man and beast. This for Brink was just getting underway;
for the wolf it was the beginning of a period of uncertainty.

Toward the middle of the afternoon the sun came out fitfully,
warming the glades with color, if not with heat. The snow
softened to the extent that at the bottom of Old Gray's deep
tracks it grew dark and wet. The wind lulled, too. Brink did not
want a warm spell, even for a day. Still, come what might, he
believed, even if the snow did melt, the ground would stay soft
until another storm. November had arrived, and at that height of
land winter had come.

Old Gray kept to his straight course until halted by the trail he
and his loafer allies and Brink and the buck had left in the snow.
Here Old Gray had stood in his tracks. Brink imagined he could
see the great gray brute, awakening to the scent and trail of man,
and their relation to him. Old Gray had crossed and recrossed the
trail, trotted forward and back, and then he had left it to continue
the straight course at precisely the same gait.

This nonplussed the hunter, who had calculated that the wolf
would deliberately set out to find what was tracking him. But
there seemed nothing sure here, except that the beast had tarried
at this crossing to smell the man tracks.

Brink took comfort in the assurance that the future trail would
prove everything. He trudged on as before. A cold drab twilight
halted him in dense forest, mostly spruce. He selected one so
thick of foliage that the snow had not even whitened the brown
mat of needles and cones under it. And here he camped. Making
fire, melting snow, and roasting strips of deer meat occupied him
till dark, and then he sought his fragrant bed under the spruce.

Next day it snowed intermittently, drizzly and mistily, in some places half filling Old Gray's tracks. The wolf, soon after leaving the spot where he had crossed the old tracks, had taken to a running lope and had sheered to the east. The hunter had signalized this change by a grim, "Ahuh."

Brink was seven days in covering the hundred or so miles that Old Gray had run during the day and the night after he had left the den on the bluff. He had run close to the New Mexico line, almost to the foothills of the White Mountains. It beat any performance Brink could recall in his experience. He must have covered the distance in eighteen hours or less; and in his wolf mind, Brink was absolutely certain, he believed he had traveled far beyond pursuit. For then he had abandoned the straight running course for one of a prowling, meandering hunt. But deer tracks were scarce and he had to go down into the range country for a kill.

Three days more of travel for Brink brought him to the spot where Old Gray had pulled down a yearling and had eaten his fill. Coyotes had left the carcass in such condition that Brink could not tell anything from it, except the mere presence and its meaning.

"Nine days behind," soliloquized Brink. "But it has showed some, an' I reckon I'm playin' on velvet."

Even the lowland cattle ranges were covered with a thin mantle of snow. Toward the foothills it deepened. Mount Ord and Old Baldy showed pure white in the distance.

Brink strode on, wed to those wolf tracks. Old Gray left a gruesome record of his night marauds. How bold he was. Yet wide apart indeed were his kills. He would travel miles away from the scene of his last attack, up into the high country, where deep snow made it impossible for hounds to follow. Brink found tracks of both dogs and hunters that had taken his trail, only to abandon it. Old Gray had the spirit of a demon. He wrote his size, ferocity, cunning, age, strength, speed, character, and history in his tracks. He was a lone wolf in all the tremendous significance of that name. For him there was no safety in numbers. He ran alone, bold, defiant, vicious. It seemed to Brink that he killed out of wild love for shedding blood. He chased stock to the very corral gates of some rancher, and in one instance he killed a calf in a pasture. His tracks showed that he played at the game of killing. Like a playful dog he cavorted beside his intended victim.

It was impossible for Brink to believe otherwise than that this wolf ran at large with an instinct only second in wildness to the one of killing to eat. Not self-preservation in a sense of aloofness to ranches. He risked his life many times out of sheer wild confidence in his mastery of the ranges. He was lord of that region from mountain to desert. Many years he had been hunted. How infinitely more he must have known of hunters than they knew of him. Man was his enemy. The heritage of hatred, descended from the primal days of mastodon, saber-toothed tiger, and giant wolf, in their antagonism to the arboreal ape that was the parent of man, must have throbbed strong and fierce in Old Gray's heart. In no other way could Brink read the signs of the wolf tracks. He flaunted his wolfness in the faces of mankind. There was a terrible egotism in his assurance of his superiority. Fear of man he had never yet known. Apparently he was as secure as a swift-winged eagle that kept to the peaks.

Brink bided his time and kept to his methodical trailing. So far all the favorable breaks of fortune had been his. The gradual fall of snow, layer by layer, instead of a sudden heavy blizzard, was especially good for Brink and bad for Old Gray. Winter had come, and snow lay everywhere, even to the slopes of the low country. The deer and turkey had moved down out of the high forests.

Some time late in December the hunter struck Old Gray's trail in fresh snow that had fallen the day before. The wolf was headed down-country and the tracks had been made in the night.

"So I've ketched up with you," ejaculated the hunter. "An' that without follerin' you hard. Wal, I reckon you'll soon know I'm trackin' you."

Brink left the trail, and journeyed half a day down into the range country, and halted at a little hamlet called Pine. Here he replenished his store of provisions. His sack of pemmican he had not yet touched. That he had reserved for the strenuous last lap of this strange race. The kindly and inquisitive Mormons of the village took Brink for a trapper, and assured him there were not many fur bearing animals left.

"Wal, if you tracked round much as I do you'd be surprised how many animals are left," replied Brink dryly, and went his way.

What Brink was ready for now was to strike the trail Old Gray would break after a kill, when he was making for a high lair to rest and sleep during the day. Brink tracked himself back to the point where he had left the trail of the loafer, and here he camped. During the succeeding week he traveled perhaps fifty miles to and fro across country, striking Old Gray's tracks several times, heading both ways. The morning came then, as much by reason of Brink's good judgment as the luck that favored him, when he fell upon a fresh trail, only a few hours old.

The snow lay six inches in depth. By the time Brink had climbed out of the cedars into the pines the snow was three times as deep. Old Gray had navigated it as easily as if it had been grass. Brink trudged slowly, but did not take recourse to his snowshoes.

The winter day was bright, cold and keen, though not biting, and the forest was a solemn, austere world of white and brown and green. Not a bird or a living creature crossed Brink's vision, and tracks of animals were few and far between. It so happened that there was no wind, an absolutely dead calm, something rather unusual for high altitude at this season. The section of the country contained almost as much park area as forest. It was easy going despite a gradual ascent.

Old Gray traveled at least eighteen miles up and down, mostly up, before he took to a rocky brushy recess. Brink considered the distance at least that far, because he had walked six hours since he struck the trail.

Taking the general direction of Old Gray's tracks, Brink left them and making a wide detour he approached on the opposite side of this fastness. He encountered no tracks leading out on that side. The wolf was there, or had been there when Brink arrived. Naturally he wanted the wolf to see him. There was no sense in trying to surprise the loafer. After a careful survey of the thicketed ridge he chose the quickest way up and scaled it.

As Brink swept sharp sight down over the jumble of boulders and vine-matted thickets, to the saddle of the ridge where it joined another, he espied a gray trotting wolf shape.

It was a quarter of a mile distant. Yet did his eyes deceive him? Not that he might not see a wolf, but that its size was incredible.

Brink let out a stentorian yell, which pealed on the cold air like a blast. The wolf leaped as if he had been shot at. But he did not run. He looked back and up. Then he trotted, nervously and hurriedly, it seemed, peering all around and especially behind, until he attained a bare rise of ridge.

There he stood motionless, gazing up at Brink. But for the background of snow the wolf would have appeared white. He was gray, with a black slash on his neck. Even at that distance Brink clearly made out the magnificence of him, the unparalleled wildness, the something that could be defined only as an imperious and contemptuous curiosity.

Brink uttered another yell, more stentorian than the first, concatenated and mounting, somewhat similar to the Comanche war whoop, which he had heard in all its appalling significance. Brink meant this yell to serve a purpose, so that Old Gray would recognize it again; yet all the same it was an expression of his own passion, a challenge, a man's incomprehensible menace to a hereditary foe.

Old Gray raised his front feet, an action of grace that lifted his great gray shape into moving relief against the background of snow, and then, dropping back on all fours, he trotted up the ridge, looking backward.

IV

BRINK HAD LONG FORTIFIED himself to meet the grueling test of this chase—the most doubtful time—the weeks of cold tracking—the ever-increasing distance between him and the great wolf. For when Old Gray espied him that morning he took to real flight. Suspicious of this strange pursuer without horse or dog, he left the country. But as range and mountain, valley and dale, canyon and ridge were all snow covered, he left a record of his movements. His daily and nightly tracks were open pages for Brink to read.

Five weeks, six, seven—then Brink lost count of time. The days passed, and likewise the miles under his snowshoes. Spruce and cedar and pinon, thicket of pine and shelving ledge of rock, afforded him shelter at night. Sunshine or snowstorm were all the same to him. When the fresh snow covered Old Gray's tracks, which sometimes happened, Brink with uncanny sagacity and unerring instinct eventually found them again. Old Gray could not spend the winter in a cave, as did the hibernating bears. The wolf had to eat; his nature demanded the kill—hot blood and flesh. Thus his very beastliness, his ferocity, and his tremendous activity doomed him in this contest for life with a man creature of a higher species.

His tracks led back to the Cibeque, down into the Tonto Basin, across Hell-Gate, and east clear to the Sierra Ancas, then up the bare snow-patched ridges of the Basin, into the chaparral of juniper and manzanita and mescal, on up the rugged Mazatal range; over it and west to the Red Rock country, then across the pine-timbered upland to the San Francisco Peaks, around them to the north and down the gray bleak reaches of the desert to the Little Colorado, and so back to the wild fastnesses where that winding river had its source in the White Mountains.

What a bloody record Old Gray left. It seemed pursuit had redoubled his thirst for slaughter, his diabolical defiance of the

ranches, his magnificent boldness. Perhaps he was not yet sure
that there was a tireless step on his trail. But Brink believed the
wolf had sensed his enemy, even though he could not scent him.
This conviction emanated from Brink's strange egotism. Yet the
wolf had roused to no less than a frenzy of killing, over a wider
territory than ever before. Far and wide as he wandered he yet
kept within night raid of the cattle range. He must have known
the vast country as well as the thicket where he had been
whelped.

The time came when the ceaseless activity of the loafer began
to tell on even his extraordinary endurance. He slowed up; he
killed less frequently; he traveled shorter distances; he kept more
to the south slopes and nearer the rangeland. All of which might
have attested to the gradual lulling of his suspicions. The greatest
of wild animals could not help forget, or at least grow less
cautious, when safety day by day wore fear into oblivion.
Nevertheless, Brink could never satisfy himself that Old Gray did
not think his tracks were haunted.

Thus tracker and fugitive drew closer together. The man,
driven by an unquenchable spirit, seemed to gather strength from
toil and loneliness and the gradual overtaking of his quarry. The
wolf, limited to instinct and the physical power endowed by
nature, showed in his tracks an almost imperceptible, yet inevitable decline of strength. Any wolf would wear slower and
lighter through a hard winter.

The sun worked higher in the heavens and the days grew
longer. The thin crust of snow in exposed places slowly dis-
integrated until it no longer supported the weight of a wild cat or
coyote, deer or wolf. This was the crowning treachery of the
snow.

Why did Old Gray stand sometimes in the early morning,
leaving telltale tracks on ridges and high points? Why did he
circle back and cross his old trail? Brink knew, and the long trail
was no more monotonous. The dawn came, too, when he knew

the wolf had spied him. That day changed life for Old Gray. He proceeded on what Brink called a serious even track. No burst of speed. No racing out of the country. No running amuck among the cattle, leaving a red tinge on his trail.

Brink halted at sunset under a brushy foothill, dark and shaggy against the cold rose sky. The air was still, and tight with frost. Brink led out his stentorian yell that pealed like a blast of thunder out over the snow-locked scene. The echo clapped back from the hill and rolled away, from cliff to forest wall, and died hollowly in the distance. If Old Gray hid within two miles of where Brink stood, that ominous knell must have reached his ears. Brink, in his mind's eye, saw the great beast start, and raise his sharp, wild head to listen, and tremble with instinct which had come down to him from the ages. No day since the advent of man on earth had ever seen the supremacy of beast.

The king of the gray wolves became a hunted creature. He shunned the rangelands where the cattle nipped the bleached grass out of the thinning snow. At night, on the cedar slopes, he stalked deer, and his kills grew infrequent. At dawn he climbed to the deep snows of the uplands, and his periods of sleep waxed shorter. Brink's snowshoes were as seven-league boots. The snow was nothing to him. But Old Gray labored through the drifts. The instinct of the wild animal prompts it to react to a perilous situation in a way that most always is right. Safety for the intelligent wolf did lie away from the settlements, the ranches, and the lowlands, far up in the snowy ridges. Many a pack of hounds and band of horsemen Old Gray had eluded in the deep snows. In this case, however, he had something to reckon with far beyond his ken.

Hunger at length drove Old Gray farther down the south slopes, where he stalked deer and failed to kill as often as he killed. Time passed, and the night came when the wolf missed twice on chances that, not long ago, would have been play for him. He never attempted to trail another deer. Instead he tracked

turkeys to their roosts and skulked in the brush until at dawn they
alighted. Not often was his cunning rewarded. Lower still he was
forced to go, into the canyons, and on the edge of the lowlands,
where like any common coyote he chased rabbits. And then his
kills became few and far between. Last and crowning proof of his
hunger and desperation he took to eating porcupines. How the
mighty had fallen. Brink read this tragedy in the tracks in the
snow.

For weeks Brink had expected to overtake Old Gray and drive
him from his day's lair. This long-hoped for event at length took
place at noon on a cold, bright day, when Brink suddenly espied
the wolf on the summit of a high ridge, silhouetted against the
pale sky. Old Gray stood motionless, watching him. Brink burst
out with his savage yell. The wolf might have been a statue, for all
the reaction he showed.

"Huh. Reckon my eyes are tired of this snow glare," muttered
Brink, "but I ain't blind yet. That's sure Old Gray."

The black slash at the neck identified the notorious loafer;
otherwise Brink could not have made certain. Old Gray appeared
ragged and gaunt. The hunter shaded his eyes with his hand and
looked long at his coveted quarry. Man and beast gazed at each
other across the wide space. For Brink it was a moment of most
extraordinary exultation. He drew a great breath and expelled it
in a yell that seemed to pierce the very rocks. Old Gray dropped
his head and slunk down out of sight behind the ridge.

On each succeeding day, sooner or later, Brink's approach
would rout the wolf out of covert in rocks or brush, always high
up in places that commanded a view of the back trail. The pursuit
would continue then, desperate on the part of the wolf, steady and
relentless on that of the man, until nightfall. Then Brink would
halt in the best place which offered, and, cutting green wood, he
would lay pieces close together on the snow and build his little
fire of dead sticks or bark upon them. Here he would cook his

meager meal. His supplies were low, but he knew they would hold out. And Old Gray would have to spend the night hunting. Not one night in four would he kill meat.

It was early one morning, crisp and clear, cracking with frost, when the sunlight glinted on innumerable floating particles of ice in the air. The snow was soft and deep. Only in shady places on the north side of rocks, ridges, or hills did the crust hold. Blue jays screeched and red squirrels chattered. The sun felt warm on Brink's cheek. Somehow he knew that spring had come. But here, on the solemn, forested heights, winter held undisputed away. Old Gray had traveled for days along the south slopes of the Blue Range; with the strange instinct of the wild he had climbed through a pass, and now he was working down on the north side.

Far below Brink saw the black belt of forest, brightened by the open white senecas, little bare parks peculiar to the region. He would see and hear the tumbling streams, now released from their ice-locked fastnesses. Lower still stretched the rangeland, a patchwork of white and black. The air held a hint of spring. Brink smelled it, distinguished it from the cold tang of spruce and pine, and the faint fragrance of wood smoke.

Old Gray was not far ahead. His dragging tracks were fresh. Long had it been since he had stepped lightly and quickly over thin crust. And in the soft snow he waded. He did not leave four-foot tracks, but ragged furrows, sometimes as deep as his flanks.

The spruce and fir were dwarfed in size and few in number, growing isolated from one another. Below these straggling trees stood out patches and clumps of forest. Brink plodded on wearily, every step a torture. Only the iron of his will, somehow projected into his worn muscles and bones, kept him nailed to that trail. His eyes had begun to trouble him. He feared snow-blindness, that bane of the mountaineer. His mind seemed to have grown old, steeped in monotonous thoughts of wolf and track.

Upon rounding a thicket of spear-pointed spruce Brink came to a level white bench, glistening like a wavy floor of diamonds in the sunlight.

Halfway across this barren mantle of snow a gray beast moved slowly. Old Gray. He was looking back over his shoulder, wild of aspect, sharp in outline. The distance was scarce three hundred yards, a short range for Brink's unerring aim. This time he did not yell. Up swept his rifle and froze to his shoulder. His keen eye caught the little circular sight and filled it with gray.

But Brink could not pull the trigger. A tremendous shock passed over him. It left him unstrung. The rifle wavered out of alignment with the dragging wolf. Brink lowered the weapon.

"What's come—over me?" he rasped out, in strange amaze. Weakness? Exhaustion? Excitement? Despite a tumult in his breast, and a sudden numbness of his extremities, he repudiated each of these queries. The truth held aloof until Old Gray halted out there on the rim of the bench and gazed back at his human foe.

"I'll kill you with my bare hands," yelled Brink, in terrible earnestness.

Not until the ultimatum burst from his lips did the might of passion awake in him. Then for a moment he was a man possessed with demons. He paid in emotion for the months of strain on body and mind. That spell passed. It left him rejuvenated.

"Old Gray, if I shot you it'd prove nothin," he called, grimly, as if the wolf could understand. "It's man ag'in wolf."

And he threw his rifle aside in the snow, where it sank out of sight. As Brink again strode forward, with something majestic and implacable in his mien, Old Gray slunk out of sight over the rim of the snow bench. When the tracker reached the edge of this declivity the wolf had doubled the distance between them. Downhill he made faster time. Brink stood a moment to watch him. Old Gray had manifestly worn beyond the power to run, but on places where the snow crust upheld his weight he managed a weary trot. Often he looked back over his shoulder. These acts were performed spasmodically, at variance with his other movements, and betrayed him victim to terror. Uncertainty had ceased. There was a monster on his trail. Man. His hereditary foe.

Brink had to zigzag down snowy slopes, because it was awkward and sometimes hazardous to attempt abrupt descents on snowshoes. Again the loafer drew out of sight. Brink crossed and recrossed the descending tracks. Toward the middle of the afternoon the mountain slope merged into a level and more thickly timbered country. Yet the altitude was too great for dense forest. It was a wilderness of white and black, snowy ridges, valleys, swales, and senecas interspersed among strips of forest, patches and thickets of spruce, deep belts of timber.

By the strange perversity of instinct Old Gray chose the roughest travel, the darkest thicket, the piece of wood most thickly obstructed by windfalls. Brink avoided many of these sections of the trail; sometimes he made shortcuts. He did not see the wolf again that day, though he gained upon him. Night intervened.

In the cold, gray dawn, when the ghostly spruces were but shadows, Brink strode out on the trail. There was now a difference in his stride. For months he had tramped along, reserving his strength, slowly, steadily, easily without hurry or impatience. That restraint constituted part of his greatness as a tracker. But now he had the spring of a deer-stalker in his step. The weariness and pang of muscle and bone had strangely fled.

Old Gray's tracks now told only one story. Flight. He did not seek to hunt meat. He never paused to scent at trail of deer or cat. His tracks seemed to tell of his wild yet sure hope of soon eluding his pursuer.

Before noon Brink again came in sight of the wolf, and did not lose it except when declivities or obstruction came between them. Old Gray passed the zone of snow crust. He walked and waded

and wallowed through the deep white drifts. How significant that
he gazed backward more than forward. Whenever he espied
Brink he forced a harder gait that kept the hunter from gaining.

All afternoon the distance between them varied from four to
five hundred yards. At intervals Brink let out his stentorian yell,
that now rang with a note of victory. Always it made Old Gray
jerk as if he had been stung from behind. It forced him into an
action that would have terminated in a leap forward had his
strength answered to his wild spirit. Then soon again his strained
efforts would sink back to the weary drag through the snow.

When the chill mountain dusk fell Brink abandoned the
pursuit for the day and made camp under a thick-branched, tent-
like spruce, his favorite kind of place. Here he had to cut the first
drooping branches, so that he could obtain head room under the
canopy. A rousing fire soon melted the snow down to the ground.
It was significant that he broke his rule of eating sparingly. This
meal was almost a hearty one. Likewise he returned to his old
habit of sitting and standing before the fire, watching the blaze,
the red embers, the growing opal ashes. He had no thought aside
from the wolf and the surroundings that insulated them. The
moon shone brightly down on a cold, solemn mountain world.
No wind, no cry of bird or beast, no sound except the crackling of
the dying fire. He seemed a part of the wilderness. When he
rolled in his blanket he heaved a deep breath, almost a sigh, and
muttered, "Tomorrow, mebbe—or sure the day after."

The next morning was not half gone before Brink caught up
with Old Gray. The wolf had not eaten or slept or rested, yet he
had traveled scarcely ten miles. But he had lagged along. At sight
of the hunter he exhibited the panic of a craven dog. The action of
his accelerated pace was like the sinking of his body forward.
Then he went on, and for long kept even with his pursuer.

The time came, however, when Brink began almost imperceptibly to gain. Brink's practiced eye saw it long before the wolf. But
at length Old Gray looked back so often that he bumped into

brush and trees. Then he seemed hurried into a frenzy which did not in the least augment his speed. He knew his pursuer was gaining, yet even that could not spur his jaded body to greater effort.

The sun set; twilight fell gray and black; dusk mantled the wintry scene; then night followed imperceptibly. But this night the wolf tracker did not abandon the tracks.

Above the cold white peaks a brightness illumined the dark blue sky. It had strange power over the shadows below. They changed, retreated, lightened. The moon rose above the mountain and flooded that lonely solitude with radiance.

The black spear-pointed spruces stood motionless, weird and spectral on the moon-blanched snow. The cliffs loomed gray and obscure. Dead bleached trees shone ghastly in the moonlight. Night, moon, snow, winter, solitude, nature seemed to grip all in a lifeless vice.

But two objects wound slowly across the white spaces. How infinitesimal against that background. An animal pursued by a human. Two atoms endowed with strange spirit down upon which the moon shone in seeming pity.

The hours wore on. The moon soared. The scene changed. A wind mourned out of the north. The spectral spruces swayed against the blue sky. A muffled roar of slipping avalanche rose from a long distance and died away. On the level reaches of snow that bright eye above could see the slow diminishing of space between man and wolf. Five hundred yards—four hundred—three hundred.

The shadows of peaks and cliffs and trees gradually turned to the other side. The moon slanted through the hours, paled and waned, and slanted behind the range. Through the gray gloom and obscurity, pursued and pursuer wended a deviating way, indifferent to Nature and elements and darkness or light.

Dawn was at hand, gray, mysterious, strange, beautiful, as it had broken millions of times in the past. The earth was turning on its axis. The sun was on the rise. In that mountain solitude there brooded the same life and death as had always been there. Five hundred thousand years before this hour the same drama of man and beast might have been enacted.

Yet hardly the same. The cave man fought the cave bear and saber-toothed tiger and giant wolf only to survive. Self-preservation was the primal law. Now only the instinct of the wolf remained the same.

Before man lived in caves he was arboreal; he descended from his abode in trees to walk on his feet and work with his hands, and fight. Through the dim dark ages forward, his instinct, reason, intelligence developed. In his four-footed foes these qualities remained static.

The meaning of that revolved vaguely in Brink's somber thoughts. But this wolf tracker had no clear conception of the great passion which possessed his soul. When daylight came and he saw Old Gray dragging his gaunt body through the snow, now only a hundred paces distant, he awoke the cold mocking echoes with his terrible yell. And the shock of it appeared to send the wolf staggering off his feet. When the sun tipped the snow-rimmed mountain far above, to bathe the valley in morning glory, Brink was gaining inch by inch.

The end of the long chase was not far off. Old Gray's heart had broken. It showed in every step he made. Sagging and lame, he struggled through the snow; he wove along and fell and got up to drive his worn-out body to yet another agony. Seldom he gazed back now. When he did turn he showed to Brink a wolf face that seemed extraordinarily to express the unalterable untameableness of the wild. That spirit was fear. If in that instant Old Gray could have suddenly become endowed with all his former strength, he would never have turned to kill his age-long enemy.

Brink's endurance was almost spent. Yet he knew he would last, and his stride did not materially lessen. Sometimes a haze overspread his eyes and black spots danced in his sight. The pangs of his body were innumerable and almost unbearable. Yet he went on.

What was in his mind? What had driven him to these superhuman exertions? The remote past was with him surely, though he had no consciousness of that. The very marrow of his bones seemed to gather and swell and throb in readiness to burst into a mighty thrill when he had proved that he was stronger than this beast. Often he scooped up a handful of snow to put into his dry mouth. His heart labored heavily with sharp pains, and there was a drumming in his ears. Inch by inch he gained. But he stifled his strange exultation.

The battle must go to the strong—to prove the survival of the fittest. Nature had developed this wolf to the acme of perfection. But more merciless than nature was life, for life had weakness. Man shared this weakness with all animals, but man possessed some strange, sustaining, unutterable, ineradicable power. Brink relied upon it. Old Gray was yielding to it.

The last hour grew appalling. Brink felt on the verge of collapse. Old Gray's movements were those of a dying creature. The hunter did not gain any more. Over white benches, through spruce thickets, under the windfalls man and beast remained only a few paces apart. Brink could have knocked the wolf over with a club. But he only stretched out a great clutching hand, as if the next moment he could close it round that black-slashed neck.

The solemn day advanced. And from the last slope of mountain in the rangeland below spread out gray and green in the habiliments of spring. The long winter was over. Cattle dotted the pasture lands.

Under Brink's snowshoes the snow grew wet and soft. Soon he must take them off. But there would be drifts in the black belt of pine forest below. He smelled the tang of the pines, warm, sweet, woody.

The irregular furrow which he trod out with his snowshoes led down over slope and bench to level forest. Under the stately spreading pines the snow swelled into wavy mounds.

Old Gray sank the length of his legs, fell on his side, and lay still.

Soon the wolf tracker stood over him, gaping down.

"Ahuh—Old Gray—you're done," he panted huskily.

All that appeared left of magnificence about this wolf was his beautiful gray coat of fur, slashed at the neck with a glossy mark of black. Old Gray was lean and thin. His wild head lay on the snow, with mouth open, tongue protruding. How white and sharp the glistening fangs.

It was nothing new for Brink to see the coward in a beaten wolf. The legend of the ferocity of a trapped wolf was something he knew to be untrue. This notorious loafer, so long a menace to the range, showed in his wonderful gray eyes his surrender to man. The broken heart, the broken spirit, the acceptance of death. Brink saw no fear now—only resignation. And for a moment it halted his propelling rush to violence.

Man and wolf, age-long hereditary foes, alone there in the wilderness. Man the conqueror—man obsessed with the idea that man was born in the image of God. No wolf—no beast had ever been or could ever be man's equal. Brink's life had been an unconscious expression of this religion. This last and supreme test to which he had so terribly addressed himself had been the climax of his passion to prove man's mastery over all the beasts of the field.

Yet, with brawny hand extended, Brink suffered a singular and dismaying transformation of thought. What else did he read in those wild gray eyes? It was beyond him, yet from it he received a chilling of his feered blood, a sickening sense of futility even in possession of his travail-earned truth. Could he feel pity for Old Gray, blood-drinker of the cattle ranges?

"Ahuh. . . . Reckon if I held back longer—" he muttered,

darkly, wonderingly. Then stepping out of his snowshoes he knelt and laid hold of Old Gray's throat with that great clutching hand.

Brink watched the wild eyes fade and glaze over and set. The long tremble of the wolf in the throes of death was strangely similar to the intense vibrating thrill of the man in his response to the heritage of a primitive day.

v

IT WAS SPRINGTIME down at Barrett's ranch. The cows were lowing and the calves were bawling. Birds and wet ground and budding orchard trees were proof of April even if there had not been the sure sign of the rollicking cowboys preparing for the spring roundup.

"I'm a-rarin' to go. Oh, boy!" shouted Sandy McLean.

"Wal, I'm the damndest best cowman that ever forked a hoss," replied the lean and rangy Juniper Edd, star rider for Barrett.

The shaggy, vicious mustangs cavorted in the corral, and whistled, squealed, snorted, and kicked defiance at their masters.

"Reckon I gotta stop smokin' them coffin nails. I jest cain't see," complained Thad Hickenthorp.

"Aw, it ain't cigarettes, Hick," drawled the redheaded Matty Lane. "Your eyes had plumb wore out on Sally Barrett."

"She's shore dazzlin', but thet's far enough for you to shoot off your chin," replied Thad.

"Cheese it, you fellars. Hyar comes the boss," added another cowboy.

Barrett strode from the ranch house. Once he had been a cowboy as lithe and wild as any one of his outfit. But now he was a heavy, jovial, weather-beaten cattleman.

"Boys, heah's word from my pardner, Adams," he said, with satisfaction. "All's fine an' dandy over on the Cibeque. You got to rustle an' shake dust or that outfit will show us up. Best news of all is about Old Gray. They haven't seen hide nor hair nor track of that wolf for months. Neither have we. I wonder now.... Wouldn't it be dod-blasted good luck if we was rid of that loafer?

On that moment a man appeared turning into the lane, and his appearance was so unusual that it commanded silence on the part of Barrett and his cowboys. This visitor was on foot. He limped. He sagged under a pack on his shoulder. His head was bowed somewhat, so that the observers could not see his face. His motley garb was so tattered that it appeared to be about to fall from him in bits of rags.

He reached the group of men and, depositing his pack on the ground, he looked up to disclose a placid, grizzled face, as seamed and brown as a mass of pine needles.

"Howdy, stranger. An' who might you be?" queried Barrett, gruffly.

"My name's Brink. I'm new in these parts. Are you Barrett, pardner to Adams over on the Cibeque?" he replied.

"Yes, I'm Barrett. Do you want anythin' of me?"

"I've got something to show you," returned Brink, and kneeling stiff-legged he laboriously began to untie his pack. It was bulky and securely roped. Out of one end of the bundle protruded the frayed points of snowshoes. The cowboys surrounded him and Barrett, curiously silent, somehow sensing the dramatic.

When Brink drew out a gray furry package and unfolded it to show the magnificent pelt of a great loafer wolf the cowboys burst into gasps and exclamations of amaze.

"Ever seen that hide?" demanded Brink, with something subtle and strong under his mild exterior.

"Old Gray," boomed Barrett.

"I'm a locoed son-of-a-gun if it ain't," said Juniper Edd.

"Wal. I never seen Old Gray, but thet's him," ejaculated Thad.

"Damn me. It's shore thet grey devil with the black ruff. Old Gray wot I seen alive more'n any man on the ranges,' added Matty Lane, in an incredulity full of regret.

"Stranger, how'n hell did you ketch this heah wolf?" demanded Sandy McLean.

Brink stood up. Something tame and deceiving fell away from the man. His face worked, his eyes gleamed.

"I walked him to death in the snow," he replied.

Barrett swore a lusty oath. It gave full expression to his acceptance of Brink's remarkable statement, yet held equal awe and admiration.

"When? How long?" he queried, hoarsely.

"Well, I started in early last October," an' I saw the end of his tracks yesterday."

"It's April tenth," exclaimed Barrett. "Tracked—walked Old Gray to death. . . . My God, man, but you look it. . . . An' you've come for the reward?"

"Reckon I'd forgot that," replied Brink, simply. "I just wanted you to know the loafer was dead."

"Ah-hum. So that's why?" returned the rancher, ponderingly, with a hand stroking his chin. His keen blue eyes studied the wolf tracker gravely, curiously. His cowboys, likewise, appeared at the end of their wits. For once their loquaciousness had sustained a check. One by one, silent as owls and as wide-eyed, they walked to and fro around Brink, staring from his sad, lined face to the magnificent wolf pelt. But least of all did their faces and actions express doubt. They were men of the open range. They saw at a glance the manifestations of tremendous toil, of endurance, privation, and time that had reduced this wolf tracker to a semblance of a scarecrow in the cornfield. Of all things, these hardy cowboys respected indomitableness of spirit and endurance of body. They wondered at something queer about Brink, but they could not grasp it. Their need of silent conviction, their reverent curiosity, proclaimed that to them he began to loom incomprehensibly great.

"Never felt so happy in my life," burst out Barrett. "Come in an' eat an' rest. I'll write you a check for that five thousand. . . .

An' fetch Old Gray's hide to show my womenfolks. I'll sure have that hide made into a rug."

Brink gave a slight start and his serenity seemed to shade into a somber detachment. Without a glance at Barrett he knelt, and folded up the wolf skin and tied it in his pack. But when he arose, lifting the pack to his shoulder, he said:

"Keep your money. Old Gray is mine."

Then he strode away from the bewildered ranchman and his cowboys.

"Hey. What d'ye mean, rarin' off that way?" called Barrett, growing red in the face. It was as if his sincerity or generosity had been doubted. "Fetch the wolf hide back hyar an' take your money."

Brink appeared not to hear. His stride lengthened, showing now no trace of the limp which had characterized it upon his arrival. The cattleman yelled angrily for him to stop. One of the cowboys let out a kindlier call. But Brink, swinging into swifter strides, remarkable even at that moment to his watchers, passed into the cedars out of sight.

Zane Grey.

ROPING LIONS
in the
GRAND CANYON

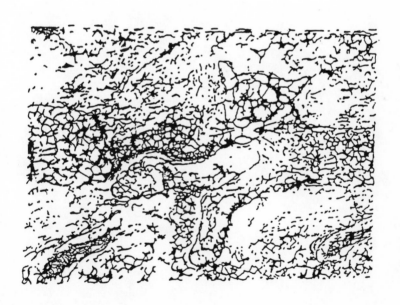

INTRODUCTION

I wish to make clear the fact that this is a story of my actual experiences with Buffalo Jones, the last of the plainsmen. My boy readers will doubtless find some of the material familiar, for in my book, THE YOUNG LION HUNTER, *I incorporated many of the incidents in the adventures of Ken Ward.*

That was fiction: this is the true story.

I am hoping that it may influence boys to a keener love and appreciation of all the wonderful outdoors of their native land.

Every boy has a heritage. It is outdoor America. Our open country, that is to say, our uncultivated lands, forests, preserves, feeding and nesting swamps, are threatened by the march of so-called progress and commercialism. What is needed is two million Boy Scouts to save some of our green, fragrant, untrammelled land for the boys to come.

The Scout movement is one of the most splendid developments of young America. Through it the future generations will learn how to fare in the outdoors, and will study the great lessons that nature teaches. To love hikes and camps and horses and dogs, to seek the wild creatures with more desire to study them than to kill, to learn to accomplish with the hands, to meet difficult situations that arise, to endure pain and privation, to cultivate strength of body and simplicity of mind—these are the things that make a good Scout.

So, in putting out this volume of ROPING LIONS IN THE GRAND CANYON, *it is with the hope that its readers will find more than mere entertainment between its covers; that the stories of lions and wild horses and deer, the descriptions of wonderful forest-land and rugged grandeur of canyons, and particularly the memory of that strange and remarkable man, Buffalo Jones, preserver of the American bison, and a great plainsman, will generate the impulse which may help to preserve our great outdoors for future generations.*

ZANE GREY

ROPING LIONS IN THE GRAND CANYON

HE GRAND CANYON of Arizona is over two hundred miles long, thirteen wide, and a mile and a half deep; a titanic gorge in which mountains, tablelands, chasms and cliffs lie half veiled in purple haze. It is wild and sublime, a thing of wonder, of mystery; beyond all else a place to grip the heart of a man, to unleash his daring spirit.

On April 20, 1908, after days on the hot desert, my weary party and pack train reached the summit of Powell's Plateau, the most isolated, inaccessible and remarkable mesa of any size in all the canyon country. Cut off from the mainland, it appeared insurmountable; standing aloof from the towers and escarpments, rugged and bold in outline, its forest covering like a strip of black velvet, its giant granite walls gold in the sun, it seemed apart from the world, haunting with its beauty, isolation and wild promise.

The members of my party harmoniously fitted the scene. Buffalo Jones, burly-shouldered, bronze-faced, and grim, proved in his appearance what a lifetime on the plains could make of a man. Emett was a Mormon, a massively built grey-bearded son of the desert; he had lived his life on it; he had conquered it and in his falcon eyes shone all its fire and freedom. Ranger Jim Owens had the wiry, supple body and careless, tidy garb of the cowboy, and the watchful gaze, quiet face and locked lips of the frontiersman. The fourth member was a Navajo Indian, a copper-skinned, raven-haired, beady-eyed desert savage.

I had told Emett to hire some one who could put the horses on grass in the evening and then find them the next morning. In Northern Arizona this required more than genius. Emett secured the best trailer of the desert Navajos. Jones hated an Indian; and Jim, who carried an ounce of lead somewhere in his person, associated this painful addition to his weight with an unfriendly Apache, and swore all Indians should be dead. So between the two, Emett and I had trouble in keeping our Navajo from illustrating the plainsman idea of a really good Indian—a dead one.

While we were pitching camp among magnificent pine trees, and above a hollow where a heavy bank of snow still lay, a sodden pounding in the turf attracted our attention.

"Hold the horses!" yelled Emett.

As we all made a dive among our snorting and plunging horses the sound seemed to be coming right into camp. In a moment I saw a string of wild horses thundering by. A noble black stallion led them, and as he ran with beautiful stride he curved his fine head backward to look at us, and whistled his wild challenge.

Later a herd of large white-tailed deer trooped up the hollow. The Navajo grew much excited and wanted me to shoot, and when Emett told him we had not come out to kill, he looked dumbfounded. Even the Indian felt it a strange departure from the usual mode of hunting to travel and climb hundreds of miles over hot desert and rock-ribbed canyons, to camp at last in a spot so wild that deer were tame as cattle, and then not kill.

Nothing could have pleased me better, incident to the settling into permanent camp. The wild horses and tame deer added the all-satisfying touch to the background of forest, flowers and mighty pines and sunlit patches of grass; the white tents and red blankets, the sleeping hounds and blazing fire-logs, all making a picture like that of a hunter's dream.

"Come, saddle up," called the never restful Jones. "Leave the Indian in camp with the hounds, and we'll get the lay of the land." All afternoon we spent riding the plateau. What a wonderful place! We were completely bewildered with its physical properties, and surprised at the abundance of wild horses and mustangs, deer, coyotes, foxes, grouse and other birds, and overjoyed to find innumerable lion trails. When we returned to camp I drew a rough map, which Jones laid flat on the ground as he called us around him.

"Now, boys, let's get our heads together."

In shape the plateau resembled the ace of clubs. The centre and side wings were high and well wooded with heavy pines; the middle wing was longest, sloped west, had no pine, but a dense growth of cedar. Numerous ridges and canyons cut up this cental wing. Middle Canyon, the longest and deepest, bisected the plateau, headed near camp, and ran parallel with two smaller ones, which we named Right and Left Canyons. These three were lion runways and hundreds of deer carcasses lined the thickets. North Hollow was the only depression, as well as runway, on the north-west rim. West Point formed the extreme western cape of the plateau. To the left of West Point was a deep cut-in of the rim wall, called the Bay. The three important canyons opened into it. From the Bay, the south rim was regular and impassable all the way round to the narrow Saddle, which connected it to the mainland.

"Now, then," said Jones, when we assured him that we were pretty well informed as to the important features, "you can readily see our advantage. The plateau is about nine or ten miles long, and six wide at its widest. We can't get lost, at least for long. We know where lions can go over the rim and we'll head them off, make short-cut chases, something new in lion hunting. We are positive the lions cannot get over the second wall, except where we came up, at the Saddle. In regard to lion signs, I'm doubtful of the evidence of my own eyes. This is virgin ground. No white man or Indian has ever hunted lions here. We have stumbled on a lion home, the breeding place of hundreds of lions that infest the north rim of the canyon."

The old plainsman struck a big fist into the palm of his hand, a rare action with him. Jim lifted his broad hat and ran his fingers through his white hair. In Emett's clear desert-eagle eyes shone a furtive, anxious look, which yet could not overshadow the smouldering fire.

"If only we don't kill the horses!" he said.

More than anything else that remark from such a man thrilled me with its subtle suggestion. He loved those beautiful horses. What wild rides he saw in his mind's eye! In cold calculation we perceived the wonderful possibilities never before experienced by hunters, and as the wild spell clutched us my last bar of restraint let down.

During supper we talked incessantly, and afterward around the camp-fire. Twilight fell with the dark shadows sweeping under the silent pines; the night wind rose and began its moan.

"Shore there's some scent on the wind," said Jim, lighting his pipe with a red ember. "See how oneasy Don is."

The hound raised his fine, dark head and repeatedly sniffed the air, then walked to and fro as if on guard for his pack. Moze ground his teeth on a bone and growled at one of the pups. Sounder was sleepy, but he watched Don with suspicious eyes. The other hounds, mature and sombre, lay stretched before the fire.

"Tie them up, Jim," said Jones, "and let's turn in."

II

WHEN I AWAKENED next morning the sound of Emett's axe rang out sharply. Little streaks of light from the camp-fire played between the flaps of the tent. I saw old Moze get up and stretch himself. A jangle of cow-bells from the forest told me we would not have to wait for the horses that morning.

"The Injun's all right," Jones remarked to Emett.

"All rustle for breakfast," called Jim.

We ate in the semi-darkness with the grey shadow ever brightening. Dawn broke as we saddled our horses. The pups

Mountain lion in dead juniper tree; Grand Canyon in background.

70

Buffalo Jones and Jim Emett packing captured cougar into a saddlebag. Note the muzzle. "The lioness being considerably longer and larger was with difficulty gotten into the other pannier, and her head and paws hung out."

were limber, and ran to and fro on their chains, scenting the air; the older hounds stood quietly waiting.

"Come, Navvy—come chase cougie," said Emett.

"Dam'! No!" replied the Indian.

"Let him keep camp," suggested Jim.

"All right; but he'll eat us out," Emett declared.

"Climb up, you fellows," said Jones impatiently. "Have I got everything—rope, chains, collars, wire, nippers? Yes, all right. Hyar, you lazy dogs—out of this!"

We rode abreast down the ridge. The demeanour of the hounds contrasted sharply with what it had been at the start of the hunt the year before. Then they had been eager, uncertain, violent; they did not know what was in the air; now they filed after Don in an orderly trot.

We struck out of the pines at half-past five. Floating mist hid the lower end of the plateau. The morning had a cool touch but there was no frost. Crossing Middle Canyon about halfway down, we jogged on. Cedar trees began to show bright green against the soft grey sage. We were nearing the dark line of the cedar forest when Jim, who led, held up his hand in a warning check. We closed in around him.

"Watch Don," he said.

The hound stood stiff, head well up, nose working, and the hair on his back bristling. All the other hounds whined and kept close to him.

"Don scents a lion," whispered Jim. "I've never known him to do that unless there was the scent of a lion on the wind."

"Hunt 'em up, Don, old boy," called Jones.

The pack commenced to work back and forth along the ridge. We neared a hollow when Don barked eagerly. Sounder answered and likewise Jude. Moze's short angry "bow-wow" showed the old gladiator to be in line.

"Ranger's gone," cried Jim. "He was farthest ahead. I'll bet he's struck it. We'll know in a minute, for we're close."

The hounds were tearing through the sage, working harder and harder, calling and answering one another, all the time getting down into the hollow.

Don suddenly let out a string of yelps. I saw him running head up, pass into the cedars like a yellow dart. Sounder howled his deep, full bay, and led the rest of the pack up the slope in angry clamour.

"They're off!" yelled Jim, and so were we.

In less than a minute we had lost one another. Crashings among the dry cedars, thud of hoofs and yells kept me going in one direction. The fiery burst of the hounds had surprised me. I remembered that Jim had said Emett and his charger might keep the pack in sight, but that none of the rest of us could.

It did not take me long to realize what my mustang was made of. His name was Foxie, which suited him well. He carried me at a fast pace on the trail of some one; and he seemed to know that by keeping in this trail part of the work of breaking through the brush was already done for him. Nevertheless, the sharp dead branches, more numerous in a cedar forest than elsewhere, struck and stung us as we passed. We climbed a ridge, and found the cedars thinning out into open patches. Then we faced a bare slope of sage and I saw Emett below on his big horse.

Foxie bolted down this slope, hurdling the bunches of sage, and showing the speed of which Emett had boasted. The open ground, with its brush, rock and gullies, was easygoing for the little mustang. I heard nothing save the wind singing in my ears. Emett's trail, plain in the yellow ground, showed me the way. On entering the cedars again I pulled Foxie in and stopped twice to yell "Waa-hoo!" I heard the baying of the hounds, but no answer to my signal. Then I attended to the stern business of catching up. For what seemed a long time I threaded the maze of cedar, galloped the open sage flats, always on Emett's track.

A signal cry, sharp to the right, turned me. I answered, and with the exchange of signal cries found my way into an open glade where Jones and Jim awaited me.

"Here's one," said Jim. "Emett must be with the hounds. Listen."

With the laboured breathing of the horses filling our ears we could hear no other sound. Dismounting, I went aside and turned my ear to the breeze.

"I hear Don," I cried instantly.

"Which way?" both men asked.

"West."

"Strange," said Jones. "The hound wouldn't split, would he, Jim?"

"Don leave that hot trail? Shore he wouldn't," replied Jim. "But his runnin' do seem queer this morning."

"The breeze is freshening," I said. "There! Now listen! Don, and Sounder, too."

The baying came closer and closer. Our horses threw up long ears. It was hard to sit still and wait. At a quick cry from Jim we saw Don cross the lower end of the flat.

No need to spur our mounts! The lifting of bridles served, and away we raced. Foxie passed the others in short order. Don had long disappeared, but with blended bays, Jude, Moze, and Sounder broke out of the cedars hot on the trail. They, too, were out of sight in a moment.

The crash of breaking brush and thunder of hoofs from where the hounds had come out of the forest, attracted and even frightened me. I saw the green of a low cedar tree shake, and split, to let out a huge, gaunt horse with a big man doubled over his saddle. The onslaught of Emett and his desert charger stirred a fear in me that checked admiration.

"Hounds running wild," he yelled, and the dark shadows of the cedars claimed him again.

A hundred yards within the forest we came again upon Emett, dismounted, searching the ground. Moze and Sounder were with him, apparently at fault. Suddenly Moze left the little glade and venting his sullen quick bark, disappeared under the trees. Sounder sat on his haunches and yelped.

"Now what the hell is wrong?" growled Jones, tumbling off his saddle.

"Shore something is," said Jim, also dismounting.

"Here's a lion track," interposed Emett.

"Ha! and here's another," cried Jones, in great satisfaction. "That's the trail we were on, and here's another crossing it at right angles. Both are fresh; one isn't fifteen minutes old. Don and Jude have split one way and Moze another. By George! that's great of Sounder to hang fire!"

"Put him on the fresh trail," said Jim, vaulting into his saddle.

Jones complied, with the result that we saw Sounder start off on the trail Moze had taken. All of us got in some pretty hard riding, and managed to stay within earshot of Sounder. We crossed a canyon, and presently reached another which, from its depth, must have been Middle Canyon. Sounder did not climb the opposite slope, so we followed the rim. From a bare ridge we distinguished the line of pines above us, and decided that our location was in about the centre of the plateau.

Very little time elapsed before we heard Moze. Sounder had caught up with him. We came to a halt where the canyon widened and was not so deep, with cliffs and cedars opposite us, and an easy slope leading down. Sounder bayed incessantly; Moze emitted harsh, eager howls, and both hounds, in plain sight, began working in circles.

"The lion has gone up somewhere," cried Jim. "Look sharp!"

Repeatedly Moze worked to the edge of a low wall of stone and looked over; then he barked and ran back to the slope, only to return. When I saw him slide down a steep place, make for the bottom of the stone wall, and jump into the low branches of a cedar I knew where to look. Then I descried the lion, a round yellow ball, cunningly curled up in a mass of dark branches. He had leaped into the tree from the wall.

"There he is! Treed! Treed!" I yelled. "Moze has found him."

"Down, boys, down into the canyon," shouted Jones, in sharp voice. "Make a racket; we don't want him to jump."

How he and Jim and Emett rolled and cracked the stone! For a moment I could not get off my horse; I was chained to my saddle by a strange vacillation that could have been no other thing than fear.

"Are you afraid?" called Jones from below.

"Yes, but I am coming," I replied, and dismounted to plunge down the hill. It may have been shame or anger that dominated me then; whatever it was I made directly for the cedar, and did not halt until I was under the snarling lion.

"Not too close!" warned Jones. "He might jump. It's a Tom, a two-year-old, and full of fight."

It did not matter to me then whether he jumped or not. I knew I had to be cured of my dread, and the sooner it was done the better.

Old Moze had already climbed a third of the distance up to the lion.

"Hyar, Moze! Out of there, you rascal coon chaser!" Jones yelled as he threw stones and sticks at the hound. Moze, however, replied with his snarly bark and climbed on steadily.

"I've got to pull him out. Watch close, boys, and tell me if the lion starts down."

When Jones climbed the first few branches of the tree, Tom let out an ominous growl.

"Make ready to jump. Shore he's comin'," called Jim.

The lion, snarling viciously, started to descend. It was a ticklish moment for all of us, particularly Jones. Warily he backed down.

"Boys, maybe he's bluffing," said Jones. "Try him out. Grab sticks and run at the tree and yell, as if you were going to kill him."

Not improbably the demonstration we executed under the tree would have frightened even an African lion. Tom hesitated, showed his white fangs, returned to his first perch, and from there climbed as far as he could. The forked branch on which he stood swayed alarmingly.

"Here, punch Moze out," said Jim handing up a long pole.

The old hound hung like a leech to the tree, making it difficult to dislodge him. At length he fell heavily, and, venting his thick battle cry, attempted to climb again.

Jim seized him, made him fast to the rope with which Sounder had already been tied.

"Say, Emett, I've no chance here," called Jones. "You try to throw at him from the rock."

Emett ran up the rock, coiled his lasso and cast the noose. It sailed perfectly in between the branches and circled Tom's head. Before it could be slipped tight he had thrown it off. Then he hid behind the branches.

"I'm going farther up," said Jones.

"Be quick," yelled Jim.

Jones evidently had that in mind. When he reached the middle fork of the cedar, he stood erect and extended the noose of his lasso on the point of his pole. Tom, with a hiss and snap, struck at it savagely. The second trial tempted the lion to saw the rope with his teeth. In a flash Jones withdrew the pole, and lifted a loop of the slack rope over the lion's ears.

"Pull!" he yelled.

Emett, at the other end of the lasso, threw his great strength into action, pulling the lion out with a crash, and giving the cedar such a tremendous shaking that Jones lost his footing and fell heavily.

Thrilling as the moment was, I had to laugh, for Jones came up out of a cloud of dust, as angry as a wet hornet, and made prodigious leaps to get out of the reach of the whirling lion.

"Look out——!" he bawled.

Tom, certainly none the worse for his tumble, made three leaps, two at Jones, one at Jim, which was checked by the short length of the rope in Emett's hands. Then for a moment a thick cloud of dust enveloped the wrestling lion, during which the quick-witted Jones tied the free end of the lasso to a sapling.

"Dod gast the luck!" yelled Jones, reaching for another lasso. "I didn't mean for you to pull him out of the tree. Now he'll get loose or kill himself."

When the dust cleared away, we discovered our prize stretched out at full length and frothing at the mouth. As Jones approached, the lion began a series of evolutions so rapid as to be almost indiscernible to the eye. I saw a wheel of dust and yellow fur. Then came a thud and the lion lay inert.

Jones pounced upon him and loosed the lasso around his neck.

"I think he's done for, but maybe not. He's breathing yet. Here, help me tie his paws together. Look out! He's coming to!"

The lion stirred and raised his head. Jones ran the loop of the second lasso around the two hind paws and stretched the lion out. While in this helpless position and with no strength and hardly any breath left in him the lion was easy to handle. With Emett's help Jones quickly clipped the sharp claws, tied the four paws together, took off the neck lasso and substituted a collar and chain.

"There, that's one. He'll come to, all right," said Jones. "But we are lucky. Emett, never pull another lion clear out of a tree. Pull him over a limb and hang him there while some one below ropes his hind paws. That's the only way, and if we don't stick to it, somebody is going to get done for. Come, now, we'll leave this fellow here and hunt up Don and Jude. They've treed another lion by this time."

Remarkable to me was to see how, as soon as the lion lay helpless, Sounder lost his interest. Moze growled, yet readily left the spot. Before we reached the level, both hounds had disappeared.

"Hear that?" yelled Jones, digging spurs into his horse. "Hi! Hi! Hi!"

From the cedars rang the thrilling, blending chorus of bays that told of a treed lion. The forest was almost impenetrable. We had to pick our way. Emett forged ahead; we heard him smashing the deadwood; and soon a yell proclaimed the truth of Jones's assertion.

First I saw the men looking upward; then Moze climbing the cedar, and the other hounds with noses skyward; and last, in the dead top of the tree, a dark blot against the blue, a big tawny lion.

"Whoop!" The yell leaped past my lips.

Quiet Jim was yelling; and Emett, silent man of the desert, let from his wide cavernous chest a booming roar that drowned ours.

Jones's next decisive action turned us from exultation to the grim business of the thing. He pulled Moze out of the cedar, and while he climbed up, Emett ran his rope under the collars of all of the hounds. Quick as the idea flashed over me I leaped into the cedar adjoining the one Jones was in, and went up hand over hand. A few pulls brought me to the top, and then my blood ran hot and quick, for I was level with the lion, too close for comfort, but in excellent position for taking pictures.

The lion, not heeding me, peered down at Jones, between widespread paws. I could hear nothing except the hounds. Jones's grey hat came pushing up between the dead snags; then his burly shoulders. The quivering muscles of the lion gathered tense, and his lithe body crouched low on the branches. He was about to jump. His open dripping jaws, his wild eyes, roving in terror for some means of escape, his tufted tail, swinging against the twigs and breaking them, manifested his extremity. The eager hounds waited below, howling, leaping.

It bothered me considerably to keep my balance, regulate my camera and watch the proceedings. Jones climbed on with his rope between his teeth, and a long stick. The very next instant, it seemed to me, I heard the cracking of branches and saw the lion biting hard at the noose which circled his neck.

Here I swung down, branch to branch, and dropped to the ground, for I wanted to see what went on below. Above the howls and yelps, I distinguished Jones's yell. Emett ran directly under the lion with a spread noose in his hands. Jones pulled and pulled, but the lion held on firmly. Throwing the end of the lasso down to Jim, Jones yelled again, and then they both pulled. The lion was too strong. Suddenly, however, the branch broke, letting the lion fall, kicking frantically with all four paws. Emett grasped one of the four whipping paws, and even as the powerful animal sent him staggering he dexterously left the noose fast on the paw. Jim and Jones in unison let go of their lasso, which streaked up through the branches as the lion fell, and then it dropped to the ground, where Jim made a flying grab for it. Jones, plunging out of the tree, fell upon the rope at the same instant.

If the action up to then had been fast, it was slow to what followed. It seemed impossible for two strong men with one lasso, and a giant with another, to straighten out that lion. He was all over the little space under the trees at once. The dust flew, the sticks snapped, the gravel pattered like shot against the cedars. Jones ploughed the ground flat on his stomach, holding on with one hand, with the other trying to fasten the rope to something; Jim went to his knees; and on the other side of the lion, Emett's huge bulk tipped a sharp angle, and then fell.

I shouted and ran forward, having no idea what to do, but Emett rolled backward at the same instant the other men got a strong haul on the lion. Short as that moment was in which the lasso slackened, it sufficed for Jones to make the rope fast to a tree. Whereupon with the three men pulling on the other side of the leaping lion, somehow I had flashed into my mind the game that children play, called skipping the rope, for the lion and lasso shot up and down.

This lasted for only a few seconds. They stretched the beast from tree to tree, and Jones, running with the third lasso, made fast the front paws.

"It's a female," said Jones, as the lion lay helpless, her sides swelling; "a good-sized female. She's nearly eight feet from tip to tip, but not very heavy. Hand me another rope."

When all four lassos had been stretched, the lioness could not move. Jones strapped a collar around her neck and clipped the sharp yellow claws.

"Now to muzzle her," he continued.

Jones's method of performing this most hazardous part of the work was characteristic of him. He thrust a stick between her open jaws, and when she crushed it to splinters he tried another, and yet another, until he found one that she could not break. Then while she bit on it, he placed a wire loop over her nose, slowly tightening it, leaving the stick back of her big canines.

The hounds ceased their yelping and, when untied, Sounder wagged his tail as if to say, "Well done," and then lay down; Don walked within three feet of the lion, as if she were now beneath his dignity; Jude began to nurse and lick her sore paw; only Moze the incorrigible retained antipathy for the captive, and he growled, as always, low and deep. And on the moment, Ranger, dusty and lame from travel, trotted wearily into the glade and, looking at the lioness, gave one disgusted bark and flopped down.

III

TRANSPORTING OUR CAPTIVES to camp bade fair to make us work. When Jones, who had gone after the packhorses, hove in sight on the sage flat, it was plain to us that we were in for trouble. The bay stallion was on the rampage.

"Why didn't you fetch the Indian?" growled Emett, who lost his temper when matters concerning his horses went wrong. "Spread out, boys, and head him off."

We contrived to surround the stallion, and Emett succeeded in getting a halter on him.

"I didn't want the bay," explained Jones, "but I couldn't drive the others without him. When I told that redskin that we had two lions, he ran off into the woods, so I had to come alone."

"I'm going to scalp the Navajo," said Jim complacently.

These remarks were exchanged on the open ridge at the entrance to the thick cedar forest. The two lions lay just within its shady precincts. Emett and I, using a long pole in lieu of a horse, had carried Tom up from the canyon to where we had captured the lioness.

Jones had brought a packsaddle and two panniers. When Emett essayed to lead the horse which carried these, the animal stood straight up and began to show some of his primal desert instincts. It certainly was good luck that we unbuckled the packsaddle straps before he left the vicinity. In about three jumps he had separated himself from the panniers, which were then placed upon the back of another horse. This one, a fine-looking beast, and amiable under surroundings where his life and health were considered even a little, immediately disclaimed any intention of entering the forest.

"They scent the lions," said Jones. "I was afraid of it; never had but one nag that would pack lions."

"Maybe we can't pack them at all," replied Emett dubiously. "It's certainly new to me."

"We've got to," Jones asserted; "try the sorrel."

For the first time in a serviceable and honourable life, according to Emett, the sorrel broke his halter and kicked like a plantation mule.

"It's a matter of fright. Try the stallion. He doesn't look afraid," said Jones, who never knew when he was beaten.

Emett gazed at Jones as if he had not heard right.

"Go ahead, try the stallion. I like the way he looks."

No wonder! The big stallion looked a king of horses—just what he would have been if Emett had not taken him, when a colt, from his wild desert brothers. He scented the lions, and he held his proud head up, his ears erect, and his large, dark eyes shone fiery and expressive.

"I'll try to lead him in and let him see the lions. We can't fool him," said Emett.

Marc showed no hesitation, nor anything we expected. He stood stiff-legged, and looked as if he wanted to fight.

"He's all right; he'll pack them," declared Jones.

The packsaddle being strapped on and the panniers hooked to the horns, Jones and Jim lifted Tom and shoved him down into the left pannier while Emett held the horse. A madder lion than Tom never lived. It was cruel enough to be lassoed and disgrace enough to be "hog-tied," as Jim called it, but to be thrust down into a bag and packed on a horse was adding insult to injury. Tom frothed at the mouth and seemed like a fizzing torpedo about to explode. The lioness, being considerably longer and larger, was with difficulty gotten into the other pannier, and her head and paws hung out. Both lions kept growling and snarling.

"I look to see Marc bolt over the rim," said Emett resignedly, as Jones took up the end of the rope halter.

"No, siree!" sang out that worthy. "He's helping us out; he's proud to show up the other nags."

Jones was always asserting strange traits in animals, and giving them intelligence and reason. As to that, many incidents coming under my observation while with him, and seen with his eyes, made me incline to his claims, the fruit of a lifetime with animals.

Marc packed the lions to camp in short order, and, quoting Jones, "without turning a hair." We saw the Navajo's head protruding from a tree. Emett yelled for him, and Jones and Jim "ha-haed" derisively; whereupon the black head vanished and did not reappear. Then they unhooked one of the panniers and dumped out the lioness. Jones fastened her chain to a small pine tree, and as she lay powerless he pulled out the stick back of her canines. This allowed the wire muzzle to fall off. She signalled this freedom with a roar that showed her health to be still unimpaired. The last action in releasing her from her painful bonds Jones performed with sleight-of-hand dexterity. He slipped the loop fastening one paw, which loosened the rope, and in a twinkling let her work all of her other paws free. Up she sprang, ears flat, eyes ablaze, mouth wide, once more capable of defence, true to her instinct and her name.

Before the men lowered Tom from Marc's back I stepped closer and put my face within six inches of the lion's. He promptly spat on me. I had to steel my nerve to keep so close. But I wanted to see a wild lion's eyes at close range. They were exquisitely beautiful, their physical properties as wonderful as their expression. Great half-globes of tawny amber, streaked with delicate wavy lines of black, surrounding pupils of intense purple fire. Pictures shone and faded in the amber light—the shaggy tipped plateau, the dark pines and smoky canyons, the great dotted downward slopes, the yellow cliffs and crags. Deep in those live pupils, changing, quickening with a thousand vibrations, quivered the soul of this savage beast, the wildest of all wild Nature, unquenchable love of life and freedom, flame of defiance and hate.

Jones disposed of Tom in the same manner as he had the lioness, chaining him to an adjoining small pine, where he leaped and wrestled.

Presently I saw Emett coming through the woods leading and dragging the Indian. I felt sorry for the Navvy, for I felt that his fear was not so much physical as spiritual. And it seemed no wonder to me that the Navvy should hang back from this sacrilegious treatment of his god. A natural wisdom, which I had in common with all human beings who consider self-preservation the first law of life, deterred me from acquainting my august companions with my belief. At least I did not want to break up the camp.

In the remorseless grasp of Emett, forced along, the Navajo dragged his feet and held his face sidewise, though his dark eyes gleamed at the lions. Terror predominated among the expressions of his countenance. Emett drew him within fifteen feet and held him there, and with voice, and gesticulating of his free hand, tried to show the poor fellow that the lions would not hurt him.

Navvy stared and muttered to himself. Here Jim had some deviltry in mind, for he edged up closer; but what it was never transpired, for Emett suddenly pointed to the horses and said to the Indian:

"*Chineago* (feed)."

It appeared when Navvy swung himself over Marc's broad back, that our great stallion had laid aside his transiently noble disposition and was himself again. Marc proceeded to show us how truly Jim had spoken: "Shore he ain't no use for the redskin." Before the Indian had fairly gotten astride, Marc dropped his head, humped his shoulders, brought his feet together and began to buck. Now the Navajo was a famous breaker of wild mustangs, but Marc was a tougher proposition than the wildest mustang that ever romped the desert. Not only was he unusually vigorous; he was robust and heavy, yet exceedingly active. I had seen him roll over in the dust three times each way, and do it easily—a feat Emett declared he had never seen performed by another horse.

Navvy began to bounce. He showed his teeth and twisted his sinewy hands in the horse's mane. Marc began to act like a demon; he ploughed the ground; apparently he bucked five feet straight up. As the Indian had bounced he now began to shoot into the air. He rose the last time with his heels over his head, to the full extent of his arms; and on plunging down his hold broke. He spun around the horse, then went hurtling to the ground some twenty feet away. He sat up, and seeing Emett and Jones laughing, and Jim prostrated with joy, he showed his white teeth in a smile and said:

"No bueno dam'."

I think all of us respected Navvy for his good humour, and especially when he walked up to Marc and, with no show of the mean Indian, patted the glossy neck and then nimbly remounted. Marc, not being so difficult to please as Jim in the way of discomfiting the Navajo, appeared satisfied for the present, and trotted off down the hollow, with the string of horses ahead, their bells jingling.

Camp-fire tasks were a necessary wage in order to earn the full enjoyment and benefit of the hunting trip; and looking for some task to which to turn my hand, I helped Jim feed the hounds. To feed ordinary dogs is a matter of throwing them a bone; however, our dogs were not ordinary. It took time to feed them, and a prodigious amount of meat. We had packed between three and four hundred pounds of wild-horse meat, which had been cut into small pieces and strung on the branches of a scrub oak near camp.

Don, as befitted a gentleman and the leader of the greatest pack in the West, had to be fed by hand. I believe he would rather have starved than have demeaned himself by fighting. Starved he certainly would have, if Jim had thrown meat indiscriminately to the ground. Sounder asserted his rights and preferred large portions at a time. Jude begged with great solemn eyes, but was no slouch at eating, for all her gentleness. Ranger, because of imperfectly developed teeth rendering mastication difficult, had to have his share cut into very small pieces. As for Moze—well, great dogs have their faults, as do great men—he never got enough meat; he would fight even poor crippled Jude, and steal even from the pups; when he had gotten all Jim would give him, and all he could snatch, he would growl away with bulging sides.

"How about feeding the lions?" asked Emett.

"They'll drink to-night," replied Jones, "but won't eat for days; then we'll tempt them with fresh rabbits."

We made a hearty meal, succeeding which Jones and I walked through the woods toward the rim. A yellow promontory, huge and glistening, invited us westward, and after a détour of half a mile we reached it. The points of the rim, striking out into the immense void, always drew me irresistibly. We found the view from this rock one of startling splendour. The corrugated rim-wall of the middle wing extended to the west, at this moment apparently running into the setting sun. The gold glare touching up the millions of facets of chiselled stone, created colour and brilliance too glorious and intense for the gaze of men. And looking downward was like looking into the placid, blue, bottomless depths of the Pacific.

With that a puff of air seemed to rise, and on it the most awful bellow of thunderous roar. It rolled up and widened, deadened to burst out and roll louder, then slowly, like mountains on wheels, rumbled under the rim-walls, passing on and on, to roar back in echo from the cliffs of the mesas. Roar and rumble—roar and rumble! for two long moments the dull and hollow echoes rolled at us, to die away slowly in the far-distant canyons.

"That's a darned deep hole," commented Jones.

Twilight stole down on us idling there, silent, content to watch the red glow pass away from the buttes and peaks, the colour deepening downward to meet the ebon shades of night creeping up like a dark tide.

On turning toward the camp we essayed a short cut, which brought us to a deep hollow with stony walls, which seemed better to go around. The hollow, however, was quite long and we decided presently to cross it. We descended a little way when Jones suddenly barred my progress with his big arm.

"Listen," he whispered.

It was quiet in the woods; only a faint breeze stirred the pine needles; and the weird, grey darkness seemed to be approaching under the trees.

I heard the patter of light, hard hoofs on the scaly sides of the hollow.

"Deer?" I asked my companion in a low voice.

"Yes; see," he replied, pointing ahead, "just right under that broken wall of rock; right there on this side; they're going down."

I descried grey objects the colour of the rocks, moving down like shadows.

"Have they scented us?"

"Hardly; the breeze is against us. Maybe they heard us break a twig. They've stopped, but they are not looking our way. Now I wonder——"

Rattling of stones set into movement by some quick, sharp action, an indistinct crash, but sudden, as of the impact of soft, heavy bodies, a strange wild sound preceded in rapid succession violent brushings and thumpings in the scrub of the hollow.

"Lion jumped a deer," yelled Jones. "Right under our eyes! Come on! Hi! Hi! Hi!"

He ran down the incline yelling all of the way, and I kept close to him, adding my yells to his, and gripping my revolver. Toward the bottom the thicket barred our progress so that we had to slash through and I came out a little ahead of Jones. And farther up the hollow I saw a grey swiftly bounding object too long and too low for a deer, and I hurriedly shot six times at it.

"By George! Come here," called my companion. "How's this for quick work? It's a yearling doe."

In another moment I leaned over a grey mass huddled at Jones's feet. It was a deer, gasping and choking. I plainly heard the wheeze of blood in its throat, and the sound, like a death-rattle, affected me powerfully. Bending closer, I saw where one side of the neck, low down, had been terribly lacerated.

"Waa-hoo!" pealed down the slope.

"That's Emett," cried Jones, answering the signal. "If you have another shot put this doe out of agony."

But I had not a shot left, nor did either of us have a clasp knife. We stood there while the doe gasped and quivered. The peculiar sound, probably made by the intake of air through the laceration of the throat, on the spur of the moment seemed pitifully human.

I felt that the struggle for life and death in any living thing was a horrible spectacle. With great interest I had studied natural selection, the variability of animals under different conditions of struggling existence, the law whereby one animal struck down and devoured another. But I had never seen and heard that law enacted on such a scale; and suddenly I abhorred it.

Emett strode to us through the gathering darkness.

"What's up?" he asked quickly.

He carried my Remington in one hand and his Winchester in the other; and he moved so assuredly and loomed up so big in the dusk that I experienced a sudden little rush of feeling as to what his advent might mean at a time of real peril.

"Emett, I've lived to see many things," replied Jones, "but this is the first time I ever saw a lion jump a deer right under my nose!"

As Emett bent over to seize the long ears of the deer, I noticed the gasping had ceased.

"Neck broken," he said, lifting the head. "Well, I'm danged. Must have been an all-fired strong lion. He'll come back, you may be sure of that. Let's skin out the quarters and hang the carcass up in a tree!"

We returned to camp in half an hour, the richer for our walk by a quantity of fresh venison. Upon being acquainted with our adventure, Jim expressed himself rather more fairly than was his customary way.

"Shore that beats hell! I knowed there was a lion somewheres, because Don wouldn't lie down. I'd like to get a pop at the brute."

I believe Jim's wish found an echo in all our hearts. At any rate to hear Emett and Jones express regret over the death of the doe justified in some degree my own feelings, and I thought it was not so much the death, but the lingering and terrible manner of it, and especially how vividly it connoted the wildlife drama of the plateau. The tragedy we had all but interrupted occurred every night, perhaps often in the day and likely at different points at the same time. Emett told how he had found fourteen piles of bleached bones and dried hair in the thickets of less than a mile of the hollow on which we were encamped.

"We'll rope the danged cats, boys, or we'll kill them."

"It's blowing cold. Hey, Navvy, *coco! coco!*" called Emett.

The Indian, carefully laying aside his cigarette, kicked up the fire and threw on more wood.

"*Dicass!* (cold)," he said to me. "*Coco, bueno* (fire good)."

I replied, "Me savvy—yes."

"Sleep-ie?" he asked.

"Mucha," I returned.

While we carried on a sort of novel conversation full of Navajo, English, and gestures, darkness settled down black. I saw the stars disappear; the wind, changing to the north, grew colder and carried a breath of snow. I like north wind best—from under the warm blankets—because of the roar and lull and lull and roar in the pines. Crawling into the bed presently, I lay there and listened to the rising storm-wind for a long time. Sometimes it swelled and crashed like the sound of a breaker on the beach, but mostly, from a low incessant moan, it rose and filled to a mighty rush, then suddenly lulled. This lull, despite a wakeful, thronging mind, was conducive to sleep.

STRANGE PARTNERS
of
TWO-FOLD BAY

OF WHALES
and
MEN

INTRODUCTION

These are really two separate accounts of the same events relating what must constitute one of the most astonishing alliances between man and animals ever known. The first story, my father's rousing tale, came from what he had learned in newspapers and magazines about some amazing events in Australia. These accounts were later corroborated by Dr. David Stead, then of the Sidney Museum in Australia. This story was not published until 1955, more than sixteen years after my father's death. At my persuasion, it then appeared in American Weekly Magazine.

The second account is my version of the same incidents, which resulted from my visit to Eden, Australia, the little town where this all took place, and after reading a carefully researched book by Thomas Mead, published in 1961 by Angus and Robertson in Sydney. Although Dad's story was by far the more thrilling, what I learned was even more exciting and meaningful to me because of the curious, almost poignant, relationship that existed among three generations of the Davidson family and Old Tom, the acknowledged leader of the band of killer whales which visited Eden regularly each fall for a span of close to eighty years.

However, my father's story does contain a few inaccuracies, the most notable being that Two-Fold Bay was not geographically as he described it; in fact, it is two huge, open, semi-circular bays— almost like extinct volcanic craters with a small, crooked tongue jutting out in the middle toward the east—which furnishes a small harbor for the vessels of the little fishing port of Eden.

Another inaccuracy is his relating that when the whales breached on being attacked, they would make a roaring sound like a bull. As we know now, almost all sea animals communicate with high-pitched squeaks because water is a much better conductor of sound than air.

Otherwise, the events of his story, as I discovered, are

amazingly accurate, and what I did was merely to document what he had related in his version. Nevertheless, perhaps the two most important facts I learned beyond what he had written were about the extraordinary intelligence of these animals (which has since been documented by many research studies performed recently with killer whales in captivity), and the fact that, in general, their longevity period seems to be as long, if not longer, than our own.

But enough of this. I'm sure that what you are about to read will capture your imagination as have few stories ever written, and it will verify the old dictum that sometimes truth is indeed stranger than fiction.

LOREN GREY

STRANGE PARTNERS OF TWO-FOLD BAY

OOK," cried whaler John Davidson, "there he breaches again." The three other men in the tiny whaleboat scanned the water in the direction of their leader's outstretched arm. Almost as Davison spoke the huge humpback whale appeared on the calm surface of Two-Fold Bay, some six hundred yards distant, engaged in a furious battle with a school of deadly orca, known more commonly as killer whales. At this juncture, the first of the accompanying boats from the little Australian fishing village of Eden came within hailing distance of their leader. "Hey Dad," yelled Davidson's son, George, from the first boat. "What happened? Did he break off?"

"No, son," replied the elder, "the whale was attacked by a school of orca. We had to cut the line."

"Aw," groaned young George. "Why didn't you hang on a little longer?"

Young Davidson's boat came up and passed his father's and went on; all eyes were intent on the fury ahead. The elder Davidson had to call twice to make them stop. The other boats came along then and the rowers rested on their oars.

Suddenly young George shouted: "They're bearing down on us."

"So they are," responded Barkley excitedly. "If they come up under us, it will be all over."

"Back away, men," ordered Davidson.

Meanwhile, the orca and the whale had sounded again and there was only an oily slick on the water where they had gone down. Then the sea opened suddenly again directly in front of the

boat. The great blunt nose of the whale emerged beyond a white
ripple, and there was a loud puff of expelled breath and then a
whistling intake. Not an orca was in sight. Young Davidson
suddenly straightened and raised the great harpoon high over his
head. In magnificent action, he cast the iron. It sped true to the
mark and sank half its length in the shiny hump. The young men
in the boat with Davidson screamed their elation. The whale
lunged and, crashing the water, disappeared. In another instant
the boat stood almost on end, its stern sunk deeply and the bow
rising to an angle of 45 degrees. George Davidson clung to the
thwarts while his comrades hung onto the seats to keep from
being spilled out. The whale line stretched out stiff and straight,
and in that precarious position the boat sped over the surface
leaving two enormous white furrows behind.

"By God," cried Barkley, "that boy has fastened onto the whale
again. What an arm. He's a born harpooner."

"He's a born fool," rasped out the father, and standing up he
cupped his hands to his mouth and thundered: "Cut that line."

But young Davidson gave no heed, even if he did hear, which
was improbable. The boat raced on and increased its speed. The
leader ordered the other boats to row hard in pursuit. It was
evident that John Davidson was deeply concerned over the fate of
his son and the others, in view of the tales related by whalers of
orca capsizing small boats and attacking men in the water. While
his companions worked furiously at the oars, he scanned the bay
ahead. They rowed a mile or more before he spoke. Finally he said
to the others, with great relief: "Thank God, they're still afloat.
There. The whale is on the surface again and the orca are tearing
into him. George's boat is up with them. The bloody fools are still
fast to the whale." In the succeeding moments while the three
boats were gaining, the whale was driven down seven times but
he was prevented from making any long runs. At last the leader's
boat came within hailing distance.

"Cut that line, I tell you," roared the father.

This time young Davidson turned and waved his hand. "Looks good, Dad," he shouted. "These orca are doing us a good turn."

"You young fool," bellowed Davidson, "they'll turn your boat over in a second."

"Dad, we were scared stiff. Two of the orca came up to us and one went right under the boat, the other bit at the line, but he only pulled. Seems to me that if these orca were going to harm us they would have done it."

"That beats me," said Barkley, laying hold of Davidson's arm. "He may be talking sense. Don't make him cut the line."

It was evident that young George could not be forced from his object. The whale and his enemies sank once more and the skiff began to sail over the water again.

In several moments the humpback rose again to try for a short blow before he was attacked and literally smothered by the pack of killers. There were at least a dozen of them. A big white spotted orca leaped high out of the water and landed squarely upon the whale's nose in what appeared to be a most singular and incredible action. Boats and quarry were soon in the lee of the headland on the south shore and well in the smooth waters of the bay. The whale showed five times at shortening intervals. Then, some miles up the bay, he began to swim in circles. The attack of the orca had frustrated his escape and exhausted him. The orca continued to harry the whale whenever he rose, and the huge black and white fellows doggedly kept leaping upon his nose. These beasts must have weighed five or six tons, and, every time, they managed to submerge the nose of the whale before it could draw a good full breath.

The fray worked into shoal water, increasing the furious activity of the orca. The whale now floundered in three fathoms not far from the shore where friends and families of the whalers had come down to see the battle. From whaler Davidson's boat there rang a sharp command: "Pull close, George. Spear him the next time he comes up." The boatmen pulled the slack line in and laid it in the bow while young Davidson stood with his ten-foot lance waiting for the critical moment.

The whale heaved up again, slowly rolling and gasping, this time the orca paying little attention to the boat in their furious attack. However, as the rowers pulled their boat closer to the whale, the orca left off their attack, but could be seen cruising around in front. As the first skiff came right upon the rolling quarry, young Davidson elevated the huge spear and plunged it into the great beast. A geyser of blood shot high in the air. The whale let out a gasping, gurgling roar and began to beat the water with his tail in great white splashes. Quickly the boatmen backed water to a safe distance.

All eyes were turned upon the death throes of the great humpback. He slapped the water with thunderous crashes. He rolled in a sea of blood. His great head came out, jaws gaping, with the huge juicy tongue hanging out. Immediately the orca were upon him, tearing the tongue out of his mouth, and then as the whale slowly sank, they could be seen biting out great mouthfuls of blubber. The whale sank slowly to the bottom in less than three fathoms of water. Presently the orca disappeared and the great humpback lay dying in convulsions in a great cloud of murky water. As soon as the blood had drifted away on the current, the second boat put down a huge hook and anchored it in the whale. Then all boats rowed ashore where the whalers climbed out to the wild acclaim of their friends and families. As far as the whale was concerned, it would be necessary to wait a day or so until internal gases built up to bring the beast to the surface. Then he could be towed ashore and cut up.

Excitement ran high in Eden that night. The capture of the whale presaged the beginning of an industry after a discouraging time of many years during which great numbers of huge tiger sharks had continually torn up the fishermen's nets, destroying the normal fishing industry along this part of the Australian coast.

Orca, the giant ancient enemy of whales, had been known along the coast of New South Wales and Two-Fold Bay for over seventy years. That is about as long as the memory of the oldest inhabitant. Of course, the killer whales must have ranged up and down this coast for thousands of years, as long indeed as whales have inhabited these waters.

There had to be a whale industry before any notice was taken of the orca and their predatory habit of chasing whales. A peculiar kind of whaling had been developed by Davidson and his men at Two-Fold Bay, probably as primitive as was ever devised by man. The whalers used what were little more than large rowboats, harpoons with long ropes, and long-poled lances with which to put the finishing stroke to the whales. Their method had been largely unsuccessful in that they had been afraid to go out into the open sea after their quarry. They patrolled the mouth of the bay until a whale came in. Then they would attack it and take a chance on being able to hold the whale within the confines of the bay. Most of the whales they sighted had been too wary, and the few monsters they actually harpooned soon departed with most of their inadequate gear. However, because of the persistence of some of the younger men under Barkley, who had been a whaler in New Zealand, and the fact that the normal fishing industry of Eden was dying, the whalers had kept up their dogged efforts.

The capture of the first whale depended a great deal upon the formation of Two-Fold Bay. It is a body of water difficult to describe. The mouth of the bay is comparatively narrow and the inlet soon runs shallow towards the upper end, folding back upon itself, to account for its picturesque name. The background is about the same as everywhere along the New South Wales coast, very rugged and wild with white sandy beaches, green benches, and forests of eucalyptus running up to the mountain ranges which grow purple in the distance. The little town of Eden is not only picturesquely situated, but felicitously named.

This particular morning the whalers had been unusually lucky

and had sighted whales only a couple of miles out and well within
the calm water area of the bay. The elder Davidson's boat was
first to come within throwing distance of one of the giant
humpbacks. Barkley, heaving the heavy iron harpoon, had made
fast to a whale and the fight was on, to the grim concern of the
older men and the yelling chorus of the younger. The whale made
off with three or four hundred yards of rope and then slowed
down. The three other boats followed, rowing as swiftly as they
could, but losing ground. But, as usually happened, Davidson's
craft was towed to the mouth of the bay. Presently the whale
came to the surface and began to thrash around in a commotion
of white water. Barkley, standing in the bow holding to the rope,
suddenly let out a yell: "Orca, by Lord," and pointed ahead. "Look,
look. See those big black fins standing up? They belong to bull
orcas. Bad luck. It's as much as our lives are worth to go near that
bunch."

Davidson and the other two men in the boat saw the big black
fins swirling and splashing around the whale, forcing him down,
and Davidson cried: "Bad luck, indeed. We'll have to cut him
loose," and he made a move with a naked blade.

Barkley motioned him to stop. "Let's wait. There's five
hundred yards of good rope out there and we can't afford to lose
it." The whale sounded and the orca disappeared. The strain on
the whaling line slackened. Presently, as the men waited in tense
excitement, the big humpback came to the surface surrounded by
the thumping, splashing school of orca. The boat was close
enough for the fishermen to hear the bellowing roar of the whale
and the vicious splashing of the killer whales.

Barkley had heard a whale roar before in its terror, but the
other men had not. It was a strange, strangling sound. Then one
of the orca leaped into the air, a huge black glistening body with
white spots, and landed squarely on top of the whale. Sounding
with a tremendous splash of his tail, the big humpback went out
of sight as did his tormentors. Again the whale line went

This photograph of Old Tom probably was taken around 1920, when his estimated age would be at least 80 years. Old Tom was the most intelligent and the acknowledged leader of the killer whale packs which came back to Eden every year starting perhaps as early as 1850. Old Tom was the last of the leaders of this astonishing band of killer whales who died in Two-Fold Bay in September 1930. In order to preserve the memory of his fabulous exploits, George Davidson and the other whalers cut the meat off his bones, wired the skeleton together and put it on display in the Eden Museum, which was started in 1938. This display still may be seen by those who visit Eden today.

Photographing whales in Mexico.

whistling off the bow. As the boat gathered momentum and rose on its stern, fairly flying through the water, Davidson leaped forward and cut the line. The boat settled down, slid ahead a few yards and finally came to a stop. The whalers, gray-faced and sweating, eyed each other in silence. Finally Barkley, wiping his face, spoke: "I guess there wasn't anything else to do, but it's hard to swallow the loss of all that fine rope and the whale, too."

"We're lucky to get rid of him," spoke up one of the other men.

This would have been the end of it had not the younger men rashly made fast to the whale again and, with what seemed the almost incredible aid of the orca, succeeded in capturing him.

That night the men of Eden speculated excitedly on their good luck.

"Men," said Barkley, "I've got to believe my own eyes. These orca are as keen and bold as any hounds that ever chased a stag. Nearly every whale killed in deep water sinks to the bottom. The orcas know this. If they kill a whale in the open sea, it sinks before they can satisfy their hunger. This bay is a trap. The orca often hang out here and patrol the mouth until a school of whales comes along. Then they deliberately separate one from the others and drive him inshore. That accounts for the skeletons of whales we occasionally find here in shallow water. But, of course, every battle with a whale doesn't end successfully for the orca. They're intelligent enough to see that we're a help. They intercepted this whale and sent him back."

Young George answered, "As the chase kept on, they showed less fear of us."

"Well," spoke up his father, "I wonder—it remains to be seen whether they'll do it again."

On the second day, about noon, while the whalers were at work cutting up their humpback, a scout came running down to the wharf to shout the exciting news that there was white water in the offing. Whaler Davidson took his glass and went to an elevated place to take a look. A school of whales was passing the mouth of the bay and one of them had already been cut adrift from his fellows and was being hemmed in and driven into the bay by the whale killers. Davidson went back to his men with the exciting information, and two boats made ready to go out.

When they were about a mile off, it was evident that there was a big school of orca and that they were proceeding with remarkable energy to prevent the whale from getting back down the bay. According to Davidson, who had the glass: "There's a small bunch right at him and a larger number back a ways in a half circle and then a line of others stretched across the bay where the water is deep."

The whale, finding himself in shoaling water, made determined and persistent efforts to break the line of his tormentors, but whenever he charged back, a half-dozen bulldogs of the sea charged him and tore at his head, compelling him to sound and turn. From the shore watchers could see the long green shadow moving up the bay and also the flashing black and white orca at his head. The pursuit in a straight line soon ended, and a ring of orca encircled the whale. He was a big humpback whale much larger than the first one, and he still had tremendous power. But he was unable to prevent the orca from driving him up the bay to shallow water. They were on top of him every moment, and as his efforts to rise to breathe were frustrated, he grew bewildered, frantic, and nearly helpless, although the pursuing orca still kept a safe distance from his tremendous tail. There came a time when the humpback slid up on his side with a crooked-fin orca the whalers had dubbed Humpy, hanging on to his lip like a bulldog. What a strange blubbering roar the whale made. It was a loud noise and could be heard far beyond the village. Presently the whale shook free of Humpy and went plunging again, round and round. He was so big and powerful that the orca could not stop him, and Old Tom, as the whalers had named the orca with the white spots, could not wholly shut up the whistling blowhole. This humpback might have escaped his relentless enemies if he had had deep water. But between him and the dark blue water of the bay were stretched two lines of menacing orca that charged him in a body when he headed towards the opening.

It became apparent then that the orca would require the help of the whalers to finish the humpback. Davidson sent out his son and a crew of four, also a second boat with four more men. The men were still afraid of the orca, but there did not seem to be any reason for this. The orca, with the exception of Old Tom and Humpy, kept away from the boats. And it was astonishing and incredible to see their renewed ferocity when the whalers came upon the scene. Young Davidson soon harpooned the whale, which lunged out and then tried to burrow in the mud at the bottom in its mad endeavor to sound. But the whale was prevented from going any distance in a straight line. He was driven around to where a harpooner in the second boat soon made fast to him. They had him from two sides now. When the second harpoon went home, it struck a vital place, for it energized the whale to a tremendous rolling and heaving and a mighty buffeting of the water with his great tail. Out the long black head came again with the white smoke from the blowhole accompanied by a strangling whistle. Three of the orca were now hanging onto his lips, wiggling their shiny bodies with fierce and tenacious energy. Old Tom cut the water in a grand leap to alight fairly on the side of the whale's head and slip off, raising a great splash. That appeared to be a signal for the remaining orca to charge in close. In a maelstrom of white and bloody water, the whale and his attackers fought a few moments in a most ferocious manner. At the end of this attack, the whale heaved up with his great jaws spread and as he sank back, the orca in a solid mass tore at the enormous tongue.

Not long after the carnage had settled, several huge triangular-shaped fins were seen headed out to sea. So far as the orca were concerned, the engagement was ended. They swam away leaving the whalers with a seventy-foot humpback, and establishing the fact for all who had seen the incident that they had leagued themselves with the whalers.

Thus began a strenuous season for the whalers and all who were concerned in the disposition of the great carcasses. The inhabitants of Eden labored early and late. Seldom did they have a whale cut up and his carcass towed away to the other side of the bay before the orca would drive in another victim.

All through June the partnership between the whalers and the orca grew more successful. The news had long since travelled all over Australia, and many visitors made the long journey to the little hamlet to verify the strange and romantic tale. During July the whalers processed seven whales, which was about all they could handle with their limited equipment. Then toward the close of that month, the whales passed by in fewer numbers until only a stray was seen here and there. When at last they were gone, the orca were seen no more. The whalers speculated upon what had become of them and concluded that they had followed the whales. They were all sorry to see the orca go, hardly hoping that they would ever turn up again. But on the first of June the next year, on the very first day the whalers went out, they were amazed and delighted to see the orca patrolling the mouth of the bay. Old Barkely expressed the opinion that he thought they were as glad to see the whalers as the whalers were to see the orca. He proved his point when Old Tom, Old Humpy, and another orca they had dubbed Hooker, deliberately swam close to the boat to look them over—as if to identify them.

The orca were back; and it was certain that the well-known leaders of the pack, and others that had been named the summer before, had returned to Two-Fold Bay. Barkely identified Big Ben and Typee, while the elder Davidson recognized Big Jack and Little Jack and an enormous lean orca without any white marks they called Blacky. In less than two hours from the time the orca showed themselves to the whalers, they had a humpback headed into the bay. In due course they drove it into shallow water where the combined energies of whalers and orca soon added another humpback to their list.

There were more whales that summer and more orca to help in the pursuit of them. When that season ended, it was an established fact that a crew of whalers had enlisted a school of whale killers to help them in their work.

Even more remarkable, on at least two occasions, the orca had driven in a whale and helped to kill it, but made absolutely no attempt to tear at the tongue, the juicy morsel that attracted them so powerfully. After the kill had been executed and the whale had sunk to the bottom, the orca had left without further molestation.

Davidson had done a good deal of thinking about this and had talked to his comrade Barkley about it. They decided that if the whale killers did not tear out the tongue of a crippled whale and otherwise chew him up, it meant that they were not hungry. The deduction to be made, then, was that this intelligent school of orca, or at least the leaders, Old Tom, Humpy, Hooker, and one or two others, cut a whale adrift from its herd, chased him inland, and deliberately helped kill him for no other reason than to maintain their partnership with the whalers.

One night Davidson saw his conclusion borne out in a startling manner. Shortly after he had gone to bed, he was awakened by a succession of loud rapid reports almost like pistol shots. He listened, wonderingly. His house was some distance from the bay, but he had often heard the splashing of great sharks or the blowing of porpoises and other marine sounds that went on in the dead of night. When it occurred again, somewhat more clearly, he decided it was a fish of some kind.

Davidson called to his son, who slept in the next room: "George, slip on some clothes and grab a lantern and go down to the wharf and see what's making that noise."

"What noise?" asked George, sleepily.

"Don't you hear it? Listen."

Again the sound rang out—short, sharp, powerful smacks on

the water. George let out a whoop and his bare feet thudded on the floor. "Sure, I hear that," he answered. "Something's up for sure." He dressed, lighted a lantern, and rushed out.

He was gone so long that the elder Davidson nearly fell asleep waiting for him. But at last a light gleamed through the murky darkness, accompanied by the rapid tread of bare feet. George entered, letting the cool misty air in with him.

"Dad, what do you think?" he burst out. "Our band of orca have brought in a big whale and some of them are lobtailing while the others are fighting the whale. Struck me funny. What would they be doing that for?"

"No reason in the world, son, except to wake us up and tell us to come down and do our part. Go wake up the men and hurry down to the wharf," he ordered, as he got out of bed. Davidson dressed hurriedly, putting on his great raincoat; and lighting the lantern, he sallied forth into the black night. Several times before he reached the wharf, he heard loud buffetings on the water. As he drew closer, he also caught the sharp splashes and quick blows that he recognized were made by orca. Then he heard the strangled obstructed puff of a whale trying to breathe. A second later came the unmistakable and fearsome sound of the whale roaring like a wounded bull.

"By Halifax," Davidson uttered. "I thought I had seen and heard everything before, but this beats me all hollow." He halted on the wharf and cast the beam of his lantern out upon the dark waters. He could see fifty feet or more from where he stood and as he watched, there came a surge of water, a short deep whistle and intake of air, and a huge orca, blacker than the night, with his white spots showing like phosphorescence, plunged in the track of the lantern to show the gleaming eye and the tremendous seven-foot fin of Old Tom. Davidson yelled with all his might. It was as if he was halloing to the orca. The orca made a plunging sound and vanished. Then out of the darkness came rapid cracking slaps of the giant tail on the water, loud and sharp as the shots from a rapid-fire gun.

Copies of paintings hung on the walls of Eden Museum depicting the battle between a huge right whale and the whalers of Eden.

Davidson stood there marvelling. The lobtailing ceased. Out there in the bay, a hundred or two hundred yards, resounded the rush and slap and roar of battle between a cornered whale and his enemies. Then lights appeared from all directions and soon Davidson was joined by a dozen men. They were excited, eager, and curious to know what it was all about.

"Our pet hounds have chased in a whale and they're fighting him out there," replied the chief.

"What can we do?" asked Barkley. "It's dangerous enough in the daytime, let alone at night."

"There's no danger for us if we keep out of the way of the whale."

"But we ought to wait until more light," objected Hazelton.

"It's a long while till dawn. Our orca have brought in a whale, and they have signalled us to come and help. We couldn't let them down now. We'll take four boats. I'll call for volunteers."

Twelve of the score or more men signified their willingness to take the risk. This was enough to man the boats. When all was in readiness, leader Davidson shouted for them to follow him and headed out over the black waters of the bay. While two of the crew rowed the lead boat, another held the lantern high and Davidson stood in the bow of his boat with his harpoon in readiness.

"Back water," he called, presently. "Steady. Rest your oars. Now everybody listen. We got to tell by the sound." From the thrashing and swishing of the water, it appeared that the whale and his attackers were approaching the boats. After an interval of quiet when undoubtedly the whale and the orca were underwater, there came a break just ahead and as the long black snout of the whale appeared, it emitted a resounding blast as loud as a steam whistle. Davidson poised the harpoon aloft. He was a big man and he easily held the heavy iron. As the whale came sliding by, he cast the harpoon with unerring and tremendous force. In the light of the lantern, it appeared to sink half its length in the side of the whale.

"Get away. Get away," boomed Davidson as he sank to his knees with the line in his hands.

With a thunderous surge the whale answered the inthrust of the steel. He leaped half out of the water. As he came down, big waves rocked the boat, nearly capsizing it. Then the whole pack of orca were upon their victim. The sounds of watery combat and the frenzied plunging of the whale united in a deafening din. Orca and whale passed out of the lantern's illumination. Davidson yelled at the top of his lungs, but his words were indistinct. The lights of the other boats came close. The whale sounded with his demons hanging on to him, and in the sudden quiet, yells became distinguishable.

"I'm fast, men, good and hard," called the leader. "The line is going out. He's circling. Better hang close to me so that when he comes round you can get another iron in him. . . . Mike, lend a hand here. They're blocking him—turning him. . . . We can risk a tow. . . . Hey, you all back there, hang close to us, it's getting hot."

Davidson's boat was now being hauled through the water at a considerable rate. The line showed the whale to be circling, but the lantern, which had been set down, cast very little light ahead. However, the lanterns of the crew behind Davidson helped. Suddenly the line slacked, the boat slowed down, the turmoil of orca and whale ceased again. "He's sounded," yelled Davidson. "Now look out." His warning cry was echoed by the men in the nearest boat. They had seen a gleam in the water ahead in time for them to row aside, just missing the blunt nose of the whale as it heaved out. Again that whistling strangled intake of breath, a hollow rumbling roar, then the surge of a tremendous body in friction against the water, and after that the swift cutting splashes of the orca and the dull thuds of their contact with the whale. The second boat did not escape an upset. It capsized and all the men were thrown into the water. The third boat sped to the rescue, and just as quickly, young Davidson, in the bow of the fourth boat, with a magnificent throw, made fast to the sliding black flanks of the whale. The two boats towed by the whale passed the others and sped into the night. Soon the orca stopped the crippled whale and killed it. When gray dawn broke soon after, the orca had left the scene of carnage and the whale had sunk.

The successful summer passed and another followed. The fame of the whale killers continued to spread abroad, bringing many people to the bay, and the little hamlet of Eden grew apace. The whaling business flourished, and there was some talk of installing more modern methods of hunting the leviathans. But nothing ever came of it. The whalers preferred their own method and the help that was given them by the orca. So the years passed bringing few changes. The older whalers passed on or moved away or gave up their work to sit in the sun and tell tales about their great experiences with the orca. Davidson's son George became the leader of the whalers, and other younger men took the place of the old. For thirty years there was little alteration in the number and actions of the orca. Led by Old Tom and Humpy and Hooker, this pack of sea wolves patrolled the mouth of Two-Fold Bay and hunted within reach of the harpoons. And as they grew more proficient in their attacks, they also grew friendly with their human allies.

It was related of Old Tom that he grew mischievous and liked to play pranks, some of which gave the whalers a great deal of concern. Several times he made off with the anchor of a small boat, dragging the boat behind him. This was play, and after a while the whalers seemed to enjoy the experience as much as the orca. But the first time that Old Tom took the line fastened to a harpooned whale and ran off with it, the whalers were frightened and concerned, and had a difficult time recovering it. There didn't seem to be any reason for this behavior except playfulness on the part of the big fellow. The remarkable thing was that this trick of Old Tom's never lost them a whale.

He and old Humpy often swam alongside the small boats with every appearance of friendly interest. The whalers never entirely gave up their fear of falling overboard when orca were around. A heritage of confidence had come down to them from the older whalers, but it applied only to Old Tom and Humpy and Hooker and possibly one or two others. The young whalers were still afraid of the less tame and friendly orca.

Most notable of all stories told by the old whalers, and handed down to their sons, was the time the orca, either by mistake or design, drove a sperm whale into the bay. Sperm and blue whales were rare along the coast, and the whaling men had given the sperms a wide berth. Owing to the superior bulk and speed of this species, and the fact that they have great teeth in the lower jaw, and habitually charge boats when attacked, sperm whales are considered most formidable and dangerous foes.

That day, two boats went out ahead, the crews composed of younger men. Then two other boats, with some experienced whalers among the crews, followed the first two and found them fast to a whale they didn't know was a sperm. The older men, reluctant to show a shy spirit by cutting this whale loose, came to the assistance of the bold young whalers. They fought the big beast all the way up the bay to the shoal water. Here again the whalers were treated to an exhibition of the amazing intelligence of the orca. When the sperm headed toward one of the skiffs, Old Tom and his partners would lay hold of the side of the whale, carefully avoiding the great jaw, and fight him and nag him until he changed his course. This was one whale Old Tom did not try to stop breathing, for a major reason; the blowhole of the sperm was clear out at the end of his nose and much nearer the formidable jaws and huge teeth than in other species of whale. As a consequence, this fight was a longer one, fiercer and harder than any the whalers had ever seen. It was owing, of course, to the superior strength and stamina of the sperm, and the impossibility of the orca's interfering with his breathing. But when the whale reached the shallow water, the whole pack attacked him and they made up in ruthless fury what they had lost in the way of technique. The men now pressed in and tried to get another harpoon in the sperm.

The whalers had noticed a number of huge tiger sharks following in the wake of the bloody mess and this fact did not lend any pleasure to the thought of a capsized boat. George Davidson's skiff finally drew in close to the sperm and George, by a very long throw, got his harpoon into the side of the whale— but it did not hold. Suddenly the sperm turned as on a pivot. The slap of his great tail staggered the boat and threw George into the water. Cries of alarm rose from the other whalers. The boat from which George had fallen passed him with its momentum, and before the crew could back water, two of the great orca deliberately swam up to Davidson. The sperm whale was still close, rolling and thrashing around, and everywhere were other orca and a number of the big gray tiger sharks. One of the men standing in the bow of the skiff with a rope yelled at the top of his lungs: "It's Old Tom and Humpy. They're not going to hurt John."

And marvelous to relate, that is the way it was. Old Tom and Humpy, who had been friends with the whalers for fifty years, swam on each side of young Davidson and guarded him until his own swimming and a rope tossed from the first boat made his rescue possible. The orca actually followed until George was safe in the boat.

The fight with the sperm was then renewed; and in time, when the whale's weakening enabled the whalers to get in two more harpoons, the fight eventually ended up with victory for the men from Eden. Orca and sharks chewed up the whale pretty badly, but they could not injure the great head which formed at least a third of this species' body and which contained the valuable sperm oil. However, several of the orca seemed to have been injured in this fray. One was seen to swim away after the others as if he were crippled.

No yarn handed down from the old whalers to the young compared to this one. And the young whalers made the most of it. From that day, Old Tom and Humpy became heroes. But when Old Tom's body washed ashore in Two-Fold Bay shortly afterward, the villagers were stunned. Some were in favor of sending the skin to Sydney to be mounted, but the whalers would have none of this. They built a memorial for Old Tom right there in Eden.

Humpy and the other orca well-known to the whalers were often seen in the ensuing years. But whales finally became so scarce that the whalers did not go out, and the orca took to other hunting grounds. Finally the whaling business waned and died, but never the romance and wonderful doings of the orca whale killers. It was said by many that the friendly orca had all died, but others thought they'd roamed on to better hunting waters.

There are men now living in Eden who will take pleasure in verifying the story I have here told. Some will tell it conservatively; others will embellish it with the most remarkable fishing yarns that were ever invented. And they say an occasional fight between orca and whales can be seen to this day off the mouth of Two-Fold Bay.

OF WHALES AND MEN

DEN IS A QUIET little town of perhaps forty-five hundred people, whose major industry is mostly fishing, some sporadic logging nearby, and a huge chip mill, located on the bay some ten miles across from the town. Two-Fold Bay itself is a magnificent open harbor with eleven beaches, most of them relatively deserted, many in view of the town. There are several better-class motels in Eden, but tourists are still relatively scarce. The only contact is by road from Sydney—a distance of some three hundred miles—or Canberra, the Australian capital city, which is one hundred and fifty miles away. But I soon learned that Eden's history does not revolve solely around its departed whaling or logging industries. In fact, a shipping magnate, a visionary entrepreneur named Benjamin Boyd arrived in Eden in 1842, and dreamed of Two-Fold Bay as a third deep-water harbor, equidistant between Melbourne and Sydney, and with a center of commerce rivalling both. One of his first promotions in 1843 was to build a magnificent hotel on the southeast shore of the bay, the remnants of which still stand today. Boyd also started a shipping run between Sydney and Melbourne with stops at Fort Jackson, Fort Phillip, and Two-Fold Bay. Furthermore, he bought thousands of acres of property on which to raise cattle and sheep, and established the first permanent whaling station in Eden, although this was before the time of the Davidsons and their orca allies. But Boyd's administrative abilities apparently did not match his vision. In 1849, the whole venture sank into bankruptcy. An administrator was appointed from Sydney and Boyd was relieved of his position and holdings in Eden. He then turned his attentions to gold prospecting, and sailed his yacht, *The Wanderer*, to try his hand at mining in California, but after a year of fruitless effort he started back. On the fifteenth of October, 1851, he stopped at the Ponape on the Caroline Islands. Here, accompanied by a native, he went ashore to attempt some duck shooting. Sounds of gunfire were heard from aboard his yacht, but no trace of Boyd was ever found when a search was made ashore. There were rumors that the islanders had killed, cooked, and eaten Boyd, but no facts ever came to light.

Later efforts were made to turn Two-Fold Bay into a shipping center, particularly with the discovery of gold at Kiandra in 1859. But the gold rush subsided as quickly as it came, and the adroit business promoters in Sydney, who did not want a rival blocked all efforts by the local residents to build a railroad connecting Sydney, Eden, and Melbourne.

And perhaps it is just as well. Most of the townspeople with whom I talked, appeared to be content to let Eden remain as it was and is today. They seem almost bemused by the stunning tales of Eden's fabulous past and particularly of the legendary whale killers—as if it were almost a lost and forgotten fable.

I visited Billy Greig who, at age ninety, is the last surviving member of the whalers that went out in George Davidson's little boats when Old Tom and Humpy were still about. But he was shy and ill at ease, so I did not press him for details of the past. However, it was Bert Eagen, the garrulous, old caretaker of the tiny Eden Museum, located in the center of the town, who gave me more than my fill of fascinating tales about the great days of the past. The skeleton of Old Tom is preserved there in its full splendor, along with many other artifacts, paintings, and replicas covering more than a hundred years of Eden's history. Of course, Bert Eagen could hold forth endlessly on any number of other subjects relating to Eden and its history. However, much of his talk about the whale killers concerned old Tom and his uncanny intelligence and obvious affinity with the Davidson family rather

Billy Grieg, last surviving member of George Davidson's whaling crew.

120

Bert Eagen, curator of the Eden Museum, built to house Old Tom's skeleton and other artifacts commemorating Eden's whaling ancestry.

than with the competing whalers and their boats. Much of what he said is also documented by Tom Mead in his carefully researched book, *Killers of Eden*, in the form of interviews with George Davidson, his wife Sarah and surviving children, and other members of the whaler's crews still living at the time—as well as numerous old newspaper clippings and photos of the killer whales that are still available in a booklet published by the museum.

By the time young George Davidson was twenty-five years old, and taking over for his father, who was nearing retirement, he was already aware that Tom was different from the other killer whales. On one occasion George fell overboard while their boat was fastened to a whale, at a time when there were hordes of huge sharks in the vicinity. Tom immediately left his pursuit of the whale, came down and swam by George Davidson to keep the sharks at a safe distance till he could climb back in the boat. Tom also had a habit which, in the beginning, was very frightening to the whalers. Often when a whale was fastened, he would grab the harpoon rope with his teeth and pull the boat toward the whale with great speed. But the apprehension among the boat crews subsided when they realized that he was only being playful. At no time did he ever act in a manner that endangered their safety.

On another occasion, a harpooned whale had escaped into deeper water and sounded. The men had to cut the last of their rope, or the craft would have been pulled under by the whale. The whalers were disconsolate because they had lost their quarry as well as many hundreds of feet of valuable rope. But suddenly, the whale reappeared about a half mile away with the killers still harassing it. When the boats caught up, they found that Tom was hanging on to the rope they had abandoned for lost.

Some time after the turn of the century, some of the other whalers began using a gun with an explosive charge in it, which had been developed to kill the whales after they had been harpooned. George Davidson had warned the opposition boats against this practice because he felt that this would upset the killer whales, and perhaps frighten them away. But the other whalers went ahead and used it anyway. The next day two whales had come into the bay, and after the first charge was used the killers were only willing to stay with a whale that Davidson's boats had harpooned. His boats were always painted green, easily identified by the orca, and after that they left opposition boats strictly alone. As a result, in all his years of whaling, George Davidson never used a gun in his attempts to subdue a whale in Two-Fold Bay.

The Davidsons also found out that when the killers would find a whale at night and chase it into the bay, they would signal to the whalers by slapping their tails loudly on the water—which in whaling parlance is called lobtailing.

As a result of this kinship with these strange creatures of the deep, George Davidson, his family, and his crew prospered. George's son, Jack, grew up and was working alongside his father on the whaling boats and the alliance kept up till the 1920s. But by this time, George and his men had become aware that things were not the same. Some of their old friends were missing, though the pack was still led by Old Tom, with Humpy, Hooker, and the Kincher, Charlie and young Ben as his lieutenants. Humpy and Hooker were showing signs of age, though Old Tom strangely enough seemed to retain his perpetual youth.

Then tragedy struck the Davidsons. Jack and his wife, Ann, had taken their dinghy with their five children out over the surf at the mouth of the Kiah River, where they had established the whaling station, to go to Eden for supplies. It was a perfect November Sunday, with a cloudless sky and a mild breeze just barely ruffling the calm waters of the bay. Norman Severs, a member of George's crew, and his wife, Elsie, had come over to the Davidson's for Sunday dinner.

But George was uneasy that afternoon—Jack seemed to be taking longer to return than usual. "Looks like a storm brewing," he said to Norman. "We've had good weather too long."

"Barometer's okay, but there was a fair sea building up when we came across," Norman replied.

"Well, I'll go down and take a look for Jack," George said.

It was only a few minutes later that they heard George's frantic voice calling, "Come quick, Norman, and you too, Elsie. Jack's boat has capsized on the bar—hurry for God's sake!"

George, Norman, and Elsie rushed down to the shore and managed to get a whale boat out onto the now thunderous surf. They reached the overturned dinghy and were barely able to drag Ann and Tommy aboard just as she and the little girl clinging around her neck lost consciousness. In another minute she would have slid from her desperate hold and gone under the waves. But there was no sign of Jack, Roy, or little Patricia.

All the boats that were available from Eden turned out to search for the bodies. The next day they found the children, but there was still no evidence of Jack. Incredibly enough, Old Tom was there, swimming back and forth where the dinghy had capsized, as if he were trying to guide them to where the body was—and he did not leave there for days on end. Only once did he abandon his lonely patrol outside the bar, when other killer whales had driven a huge humpback into the harbor. The fight was long and frenzied, but eventually the injured whale managed to reach the open water and escape. Old Tom immediately returned to his vigil at the bar. After five days, they began to believe that the sharks had indeed gotten Jack. But Old Tom was still out there patrolling, so perhaps there was hope.

On the sixth day, Bill Greig and Archer Davidson, two of George's men, discovered Jack's body very close to where Tom had been circling. The next day the Davidsons took Jack's body in their launch out over the bar to Eden for the funeral. Incredibly, Old Tom was still there, and followed the launch all the way over to Eden. When the body, in its simple wooden casket, was finally lifted onto the dock, Tom made a circle as if to salute them, then turned out and headed toward the open sea. That was the last they saw of him until the following May at the start of another winter whaling season. George often thought about this episode in later years, particularly after Old Tom's death, with a mixture of sadness and near reverence. Tom had then become a member of the family as much as Sarah, his other surviving children, and his grandchildren.

But somehow, after Jack's death, things were no longer the same. While George Davidson whaled several more years with casual crews, he had lost his enthusiasm since the death of his son. Furthermore, the whaling they had known was just about over. For one thing, the killers seemed to be dying off one by one. The pack had dwindled down to Old Tom, Humpy, and a few of the younger orca. Then Humpy disappeared. Alex and Bill Greig saw him for the last time when fishing one day near South Head, and they knew Humpy would not come back for another fishing season. He was like a feeble old man taking his last journey to the Antarctic, which was the only home he knew.

The next winter, Old Tom came back alone. Even though many whales passed the bay, and there were younger orcas to lead, he refused to go out and round them up. He was no longer interested in how many of them there were. He would go down to the river mouth and flop about as he had done in his more active days, when summoning up the whalers to come for their quarry. Suddenly—though it seemed hard to believe—Old Tom was dead. It was a lonely, cold, early spring day—September 17, 1930—when Tom's body was spotted and towed ashore by George and his crew. There were many ideas brought forth as to what to do with the body. Some thought it would be best to have it mounted. But George, himself, decided to preserve the skeleton, in the hope that eventually a museum could be built to house it—as was finally done in 1938.

In retrospect, one can only wonder what kind of intelligence these great mammals really possessed. The killer whale had been venerated by primitive tribes all over the seas long before civilization as we know it began. Even in Eden, there is a legend about a fierce Polynesian tribe that lived and disappeared long before the aboriginals, who literally worshipped the orca and believed that if they lived heroic lives they would be reincarnated as killer whales. Indians in British Columbia have woven eyes and fins of the orca into their ceremonial blankets, but only the greatest chiefs could wear such a covering with the full whale woven into its design. There seems to be no comparable reverence known for any other sea creature. Though we are only beginning to find out how the dolphin and the orca think, some of the facts presented in this story should be of help to scientists in their investigations, as well as of interest to any lover of the wild. For one thing, the orca appears to possess a life span similar to, if not greater than our own. Their method of communication is similar in its complexity and organization to that of the dolphins, which have only recently begun to be studied. That killer whales, as have the dolphins, can develop a strong sentimental attachment to human beings seems to have been verified here as well.

There are, of course, the skeptics who would attribute all these events to a form of conditioning rather than independent thinking. Killer whales, dolphins, dogs, and apes have been trained by humans to develops superior organizational abilities as a result of conditioning. But in this case, the whales trained themselves. And what kind of conditioning could explain Tom's behavior after Jack Davidson's tragic accident, particularly when he followed the launch with Jack's body all the way to Eden, almost as if to pay his respects before the funeral. Was it instinct which kept him patrolling at the mouth of the Kiah River for days until Jack's body was found? And what brought him back to Two-Fold Bay when he knew his own death was near? Was it because he knew the waters were safer there from the sharks who were the inevitable enemy of old and crippled killers? Or was it, because he had lost all of his old friends, that he came back to the one place where he knew other friends were waiting? Who can tell?

Whatever speculations one can make about the motivations or

intelligence of the orca, I think few can deny that this tale—along with the legends about the dolphin, Pelorus Jack, who for more than forty years is reputed to have guided literally hundreds of sailing vessels through the treacherous reefs which separate New Zealand's North Island from the South Island—ranks well up among the greatest sea stories of all time.

One of Eden's eleven magnificently unspoiled beaches.

THE LAND
of the
WILD MUSK-OX

INTRODUCTION

The adventuring spirit of the English pioneers brought them to many strange and dangerous lands. None was stranger than the vast snowy landscapes of the Frozen North, and no pioneers bolder than those who went forth across the frozen plains and into the great green cathedral aisles of the forest in search of the treasure of fur and game that was the wealth of the Arctic lands. Some traded for caribou, many for beaver, marten, mink and fox.

This is the tale of an American plainsman resolved to capture and tame the mighty musk-ox, and the tale of his struggle against an unforgiving Nature and against the religious taboos of the Indians.

LOREN GREY

THE LAND OF THE WILD MUSK OX

I

T WAS A WAITING DAY at Fort Chippewayan. The lonesome, far-northern Hudson's Bay Trading Post seldom saw much life. Tipis dotted he banks of the Slave River and lines of blanketed Indians paraded its shores. Near the boat landing a group of chiefs, grotesque in semi-barbaric, semi-civilized splendor, but black-browed, austere-eyed, stood in savage dignity with folded arms and high-held heads. Lounging on the grassy bank were white men, traders, trappers, and officials of the post.

All eyes were on the distant curve of the river where, as it lost itself in a fine-fringed bend of dark green, white-glinting waves danced and fluttered. A June sky lay blue in the majestic stream; ragged, spear-topped, dense green trees massed down to the water; beyond rose bold, balk-knobbed hills, in remote purple relief.

A long Indian arm stretched south. The waiting eyes discerned a black speck on the green, and watched it grow. A flatboat, with a man standing to the oars, bore down swiftly.

Not a red hand, nor a white one, offered to help the voyager in the difficult landing. The oblong, clumsy, heavily laden boat surged with the current and passed the dock despite the boatman's efforts. He swung his craft in below upon a bar and roped it fast to a tree. The Indians crowded above him on the bank. The boatman raised his powerful form erect, lifted a bronzed face which seemed set in craggy hardness, and cast from narrow eyes a keen, cool glance on those above. The silvery gleam in his fair hair told of years.

Silence, impressive as it was ominous, broke only to the rattle of camping paraphernalia, which the voyager threw to a level, grassy bench on the bank. Evidently this unwelcome visitor had journeyed from afar, and his boat, sunk deep into the water with its load of barrels, boxes and bags, indicated that the journey had only begun. Significant, too, were a couple of long Winchester rifles shining on a tarpaulin.

The cold-faced crowd stirred and parted to permit the passage of a tall, thin, gray personage of official bearing, in a faded military coat.

"Are you the musk-ox hunter?" he asked, in tones that contained no welcome.

The boatman greeted this peremptory interlocutor with a cool laugh—a strange laugh, in which the muscles of his face appeared to play no part.

"Yes, I am the man," he said.

"The chiefs of the Chippewayan and Great Slave tribes have been apprised of your coming. They have held council and are here to speak with you."

At a motion from the commandant, the line of chieftains piled down to the level bench and formed a half-circle before the voyager. To a man who had stood before grim Sitting Bull and noble Black Thunder of the Sioux, and faced the falcon-eyed Geronimo, and glanced over the sights of a rifle at gorgeous-feathered, wild, free Comanches, this semi-circle of savages—lords of the north—was a sorry comparison. Bedaubed and betrinketed, slouchy and slovenly, these low-statured chiefs belied in appearance their scorn-bright eyes and lofty mien. They made a sad group.

One who spoke in unintelligible language, rolled out a haughty, sonorous voice over the listening multitude. When he had finished, a half-breed interpreter, in the dress of a white man, spoke at a signal from the commandant.

"He says listen to the great orator of the Chippewayan. He has summoned all the chiefs of the tribes south of Great Slave Lake. He has held council. The cunning of the paleface hunter who comes to take the musk-oxen, is well known. Let the paleface hunter return to his own hunting grounds; let him turn his face from the north. Never will the chiefs permit the white man to take musk-oxen alive from their country. The Ageter, the musk-ox, is their god. He gives them food and fur. He will never come back if he is taken away, and the reindeer will follow him. The chiefs and their people would starve. They command the paleface hunter to go back. They cry Naza! Naza! Naza!"

"Say, for a thousand miles, I've heard that word Naza!" returned the hunter, with mingled curiosity and disgust. "At Edmonton Indian runners started ahead of me, and every village I struck the redskins would crowd round me and an old chief would harangue me, and motion me back, and point north with Naza! Naza! Naza! What does it mean?"

"No white man knows, no Indian will tell," answered the interpreter. "The traders think it means the Great Slave, the North Star, the North Spirit, the North Wind, the North Lights and Ageter, the musk-ox god."

"Well, say to the chiefs to tell Ageter I have been four moons on the way after some of his little Ageters, and I'm going to keep on after them."

"Hunter, you are most unwise," broke in the commandant, in his officious voice. "The Indians will never permit you to take a musk-ox alive from the north. They worship him, pray to him. It is a wonder you have not been stopped."

"Who'll stop me?"

"The Indians. They will kill you if you do not turn back."

"Faugh! to tell an American plainsman that!" The hunter paused a steady moment, with his eyelids narrowing over slits of blue fire. "There is no law to keep me out, nothing but Indian superstition and the greed of Hudson's Bay people. And I am an old fox, not to be fooled by pretty baits. For years the officers of this fur-trading company have tried to keep out explorers. Even Sir John Franklin, an Englishman, could not buy food of them. The policy of the company is to side with the Indians, to keep out traders and trappers. Why? So they can keep on cheating the poor savages out of clothing and food by trading a few trinkets and blankets, a little tobacco and rum for millions of dollars worth of furs. Have I failed to hire man after man, Indian after Indian, not to know why I cannot get a helper? Have I, a plainsman, come a thousand miles alone to be scared by you, or a lot of craven Indians? Have I been dreaming of musk-oxen for forty years, to slink south now, when I begin to feel the north? Not I."

Deliberately, every chief, with the sound of a hissing snake, spat in the hunter's face. He stood immovable while they perpetrated the outrage, then calmly wiped his cheeks, and in his strange, cool voice addressed the interpreter.

"Tell them thus they show their true qualities, to insult in council. Tell them they are not chiefs, but dogs. Tell them they are not even squaws, only poor, miserable, starved dogs. Tell them I turn my back on them. Tell them the paleface has fought real chiefs, fierce, bold, like eagles, and he turns his back on dogs. Tell them he is the one who could teach them to raise the musk-oxen and the reindeer, and to keep out the cold and the wolf. But they are blinded. Tell them the hunter goes north."

Through the council of chiefs ran a low mutter, as of gathering thunder.

True to his word, the hunter turned his back on them. As he brushed by, his eye caught a gaunt savage slipping from the boat. At the hunter's stern call, the Indian leaped ashore, and started to run. He had stolen a parcel, and would have succeeded in eluding its owner but for an unforseen obstacle, as striking as it was unexpected.

A white man of colossal stature had stepped in the chief's passage, and laid two great hands on him. Instantly the parcel flew from the Indian, and he spun in the air to fall into the river with a sounding splash. Yells signalled the surprise and alarm caused by this unexpected incident. The Indian frantically swam to the shore. Whereupon the champion of the stranger in a strange land lifted a bag, which gave forth a musical clink of steel, and throwing it with the camp articles on the grassy bench, he extended a huge, friendly hand.

"My name is Rea," he said in deep, cavernous tones.

"Mine is Jones," replied the hunter, and right quickly did he grip the proffered hand. He saw in Rea a giant, of whom he was but a stunted shadow. Six and one-half feet Rea stood, with yard-wide shoulders, a hulk of bone and brawn. His ponderous, shaggy head rested on a bull neck. His broad face, with its low forehead, its close-shut mastiff under jaw, its big, opaque eyes, pale and cruel as those of a jaguar, marked him a man of terrible brute force.

"Free-trader!" called the commandant. "Better think twice before you join fortunes with the musk-ox hunter."

"To hell with you an' your rantin', dog-eared redskins!" cried Rea. "I've run agin a man of my own kind, a man of my own country, an' I'm goin' with him."

With this he thrust aside some encroaching, gaping Indians so unconcernedly and ungently that they sprawled upon the grass.

Slowly the crowd mounted and once more lined the bank.

Jones realized that by some late-turning stroke of fortune he had fallen in with one of the few free-traders of the province. These free-traders, from the very nature of their calling—which was to defy the fur company, and to trap and trade on their own account—were a hardy and intrepid class of men. Rea's worth to Jones exceeded that of a dozen ordinary men. He knew the ways of the north, the language of the tribes, the habits of the animals, the handling of dogs, the uses of food and fuel. Moreover, it soon appeared that he was a carpenter and blacksmith.

"There's my kit," he said, dumping the contents of his bag. It consisted of a bunch of steel traps, some tools, a broken ax, a box of miscellaneous things such as trappers use, and a few articles of flannel. "Thievin' redskins," he added, in explanation of his poverty. "Not much of an outfit, but I'm the man for you. Besides, I had a pal once who knew you on the plains, called you 'Buff' Jones. Old Jim Bent he was."

"I recollect Jim," said Jones. "He went down in Custer's last charge. So you were Jim's pal. That'd be a recommendation if you needed one. But the way you chucked the Indian overboard got me."

Rea soon manifested himself as a man of few words and much action. With the planks Jones had on board, he heightened the stern and bow of the boat to keep out the beating waves in the rapids; he fashioned a steering gear and a less-awkward set of oars, and shifted the cargo so as to make more room in the craft.

"Buff, we're in for a storm. Set up a tarpaulin an' make a fire. We'll pretend to camp tonight. These Indians won't dream we'd try to run the river after dark, and we'll slip by undercover."

The sun glazed over; clouds moved up from the north; a cold wind swept the tips of the spruces, and rain commenced to drive in gusts. By the time it was dark not an Indian showed himself. They were housed from the storm. Lights twinkled in the tipis and the big log cabins of the trading company. Jones scouted round till pitchy black night, when a freezing, pouring blast sent him back to the protection of the tarpaulin. When he got there he found that Rea had taken it down and awaited him. "Off!" said the free-trader; and with no more noise than a drifting feather the boat swung into the current and glided down till the twinkling fires no longer accentuated the darkness.

By night, the river, in common with all swift rivers, had a sullen voice, murmuring its hurry, its restraint, its menace, its meaning. The two boatmen, one at the steering gear, one at the oars, faced the pelting rain and watched the dark line of trees. The craft slid noiselessly onward into the gloom.

Into Jones's ears, above the storm, poured another sound, a

steady, muffled rumble, like the roll of giant chariot wheels. It had come to be a familiar roar to him, and the only thing which, in his long life of hazard, had ever sent the cold, prickling, tight shudder over his warm skin. Many times on the Athabasca that rumble had presaged the dangerous and dreaded rapids.

"Hell Bend Rapids!" shouted Rea. "Bad water, but no rocks."

The rumble expanded to a roar, the roar to a boom that charged the air with heaviness, with a dreamy burr. The whole indistinct world appeared to be moving to the lash of wind, to the sound of rain, to the roar of the river. The boat shot down and sailed aloft, met shock on shock, breasted leaping dim white waves, and in a hollow, unearthly blend of watery sounds, rode on and on, buffeted, tossed, pitched into a black chaos that yet gleamed with obscure shrouds of light. Then the convulsive stream shrieked out a last defiance, changed its course abruptly to slow down and drown the sound of rapids in muffling distance. Once more the craft swept on smoothly, to the drive of the wind and the rush of the rain.

By midnight, the storm cleared. Murky clouds split to show shining, blue-white stars and a fitful moon, that silvered the crests of the spruces and sometimes hid like a gleaming, black-threaded pearl behind the dark branches.

Jones, a plainsman all his days, wonderingly watched the moon-blanched water. He saw it shade and darken under shadowy walls of granite, where it swelled with hollow song and gurgle. He heard again the far-off rumble, faint on the night wind. High cliff banks appeared, walled out the mellow light, and the river suddenly narrowed. Yawning holes, whirling pools of a second, opened with a gurgling suck and raced with the boat.

On the craft flew. Far ahead, a long, declining plane of jumping frosted waves played dark and white with the moonbeams. The Slave plunged to his freedom, down his rivers, stone-spiked bed, knowing no patient eddy, and white-wreathed his dark, shiny rocks in spume and spray.

II

A FAR CRY IT WAS from bright June at Fort Chippewayan to dim
October on Great Slave Lake.

Two long, laborious months Rea and Jones threaded the
crooked shores of the great inland sea, halting at the extreme
northern end, where a plunging outlet formed the source of a
river. Here they found a stone chimney and fireplace standing
among the darkened, decayed ruins of a cabin.

"We mustn't lose no time," said Rea. "I feel the winter in the
wind. An' see how dark the days are gettin' on us."

"I'm for hunting musk-oxen," replied Jones.

"Man, we're racin' the northern night; we're in the land of the
midnight sun. Soon we'll be shut in for seven months. A cabin we
want, an' wood, an' meat."

A forest of stunted spruce trees edged on the lake, and soon its
dreary solitudes ran to the strokes of axes. The trees were small
and uniform in size. Black stumps protruded, here and there,
from the ground showing work of the steel in time gone by. Jones
observed that the living trees were no larger in diameter than the
stumps, and questioned Rea in regard to the difference in age.

"Cut twenty-five, mebbe fifty years ago," said the trapper.

"But the living trees are no bigger."

"Trees an' things don't grow fast in the northland."

They erected a fifteen-foot cabin round the stone chimney,
roofed it with the poles and branches of spruce and a layer of
sand. In digging near the fireplace Jones unearthed a rusty file and
the head of a whisky keg, upon which was a sunken word in
unintelligible letters.

"We've found the place," said Rea. "Franklin built a cabin here
in 1819. An' in 1833, Captain Back wintered here when he was in
search of the vessel *Fury*. It was those explorin' parties thet cut
the trees. I seen an Indian sign out there, made last winter, I
reckon; but Indians never cut down no trees."

The hunters completed the cabin, piled cords of firewood outside, stowed away the kegs of dried fish and fruits, the sacks of flour, boxes of crackers, canned meats and vegetables, sugar, salt, coffee, tobacco—all of the cargo; then took the boat apart and carried it up the bank, which labor took them less than a week.

Jones found sleeping in the cabin, despite the fire, uncomfortably cold, because of the wide chinks between the logs. It was hardly better than sleeping under the swaying spruces. When he essayed to stop up the cracks—a task by no means easy, considering the lack of material—Rea laughed his short, easy "Ho! Ho!" and stopped him with the word "Wait." Every morning the green ice extended farther out into the lake; the sun paled dim and dimmer; the nights grew colder. On October 8th, the thermometer registered several degrees below zero; it fell a little more next night and continued to fall.

"Ho! Ho!" cried Rea. "She's struck the toboggan, an' presently she'll commence to slide. Come on, Buff, we've work to do."

He caught up a bucket, made for their hole in the ice, rebroke a six-inch layer, the freeze of a few hours, and filling his bucket, returned to the cabin. Jones had no inkling of the trapper's intention, and wonderingly he filled his own bucket with the icy water and followed.

By the time he had reached the cabin, a matter of some thirty or forty paces, the water no longer splashed from his pail, for a thin film of ice prevented. Rea stood fifteen feet from the cabin, his back to the wind, and threw the water. Some of it froze in the air, most of it froze on the logs. The simple plan of the trapper to encase the cabin with ice was easily divined. All day the men worked, ceasing only when the cabin resembled a glistening mound. It had not a sharp corner nor a crevice. Inside it was warm and snug, and as light as when the chinks were open.

A slight moderation of the weather brought the snow. Such snow. A blinding white flutter of great flakes, as large as feathers. All day they rustled softly; all night they swirled, sweeping, seeping, brushing against the cabin. "Ho Ho!" roared Rea. "'Tis good; let her snow, an' the reindeer will migrate. We'll have fresh meat." The sun shone again but not brightly. A nipping wind cut down out of the frigid north and crusted the snow. The third night following the storm, when the hunters lay snug under their blankets, a commotion outside aroused them.

"Indians," said Rea, "come north for reindeer."

Half the night, shouting and yelling, barking dogs, hauling of sleds and cracking of dried-skin tipis murdered sleep for those in the cabin. In the morning the level plain and edge of the forest held an Indian village. Caribou hides, strung on forked poles, constituted tent-like habitations with no distinguishable doors. Fires smoked in the holes in the snow. Not till late in the day did any life manifest itself round the tipis, and then a group of children, poorly clad in ragged pieces of blankets and skins, gaped at Jones. He saw their pinched, brown faces, staring, hungry eyes, naked legs and throats, and noted particularly their dwarfish size. When he spoke they fled precipitously a little way, then turned. He called again, and all ran except one small lad. Jones went into the cabin and came out with a handful of sugar in square lumps.

"Yellow Knife Indians," said Rea. "A starved tribe! We're in for it."

Jones made motions to the lad, but he remained still, as if transfixed, and his black eyes stared wonderingly.

"*Molar nasu* (white man good)," said Rea.

The lad came out of his trance and looked back at his companions, who edged nearer. Jones ate the lump of sugar, then handed one to the little Indian. He took it gingerly, put it into his mouth and immediately jumped up and down.

"*Hoppieshampoolie, Hoppieshampoolie!*" he shouted to his brothers and sisters. They came on the run.

"Think he means sweet salt," interpreted Rea. "Of course, these beggars never tasted sugar."

The band of youngsters trooped round Jones, and after tasting the white lumps, shrieked in such delight that the braves and squaws shuffled out of the tipis.

In all his days, Jones had never seen such miserable Indians. Dirty blankets hid all their person, except straggling, black hair, hungry, wolfish eyes and moccasined feet. They crowded into the path before the cabin door and mumbled and stared and waited. No dignity, no brightness, no suggestions of friendliness marked this peculiar attitude.

"Starved!" exclaimed Rea. "They've come to the lake to invoke the Great Spirit to send the reindeer. Buff, whatever you do, don't feed them. If you do, we'll have them on our hands all winter. It's cruel, but, man, we're in the north!"

Notwithstanding the practical trapper's admonition, Jones could not resist the pleading of the children. He could not stand by and see them starve. After ascertaining there was absolutely nothing to eat in the tipis, he invited the little ones into the cabin, and made a great pot of soup, into which he dropped compressed biscuits. The savage children were like wildcats. Jones had to call in Rea to assist him in keeping the famished little aborigines from tearing each other to pieces. When finally they were all fed, they had to be driven out of the cabin.

"That's new to me," said Jones. "Poor little beggars!"

Rea doubtfully shook his shaggy head.

Next day Jones traded with the Yellow Knives. He had a goodly number of baubles, besides blankets, gloves, and boxes of canned goods, which he had brought for such trading. He secured a dozen of the large-boned, white and black Indian dogs—huskies, Rea called them—two long sleds with harness and several pairs of snowshoes. This trade made Jones rub his hands in satisfaction, for during all the long journey north he had failed to barter for such cardinal necessities to the success of his venture.

"Better have doled out the grub to them in rations," grumbled Rea.

Twenty-four hours sufficed to show Jones the wisdom of the trapper's words, for in just that time the crazed, ignorant savages had glutted the generous store of food, which should have lasted them for weeks. The next day they were begging at the cabin door. Rea cursed and threatened them with his fists, but they returned again and again.

Days passed. All the time, in light and dark, the Indians filled the air with dismal chant and doleful incantations to the Great Spirit, and the tum! tum! tum! of tomtoms, a specific feature of their wild prayer for food.

But the white monotony of the rolling land and level lake remained unbroken. The reindeer did not come. The days became shorter, dimmer, darker. The mercury kept on the slide.

Forty degrees below zero did not trouble the Indians. They stamped till they dropped, and sang till their voices vanished, and beat the tomtoms everlastingly. Jones fed the children once each day, against the trapper's advice.

One day, while Rea was absent, a dozen braves succeeded in forcing an entrance, and clamored so fiercely, and threatened so desperately, that Jones was on the point of giving them food when the door opened to admit Rea.

With a glance he saw the situation. He dropped the bucket he carried, threw the door wide open and commenced action. Because of his great bulk he seemed slow, but every blow of his sledge-hammer fist knocked a brave against the wall, or through the door into the snow. When he could reach two savages at once, by way of diversion, he swung their heads together with a crack. They dropped like dead things. Then he handled them as if they were sacks of corn, pitching them out into the snow. In two minutes, the cabin was clear. He banged the door and slipped the bar in place.

"Buff, I'm goin' to get mad at these thievin' redskins some day," he said gruffly. The expanse of his chest heaved slightly, like the slow swell of a calm ocean, but there was no other indication of unusual exertion.

Jones laughed, and again gave thanks for the comradeship of this strange man.

Shortly afterward, he went out for wood, and as usual scanned the expanse of the lake. The sun shone mistier and wanner, and frost feathers floated in the air. Sky and sun and plain and lake— all were gray. Jones fancied he saw a distant moving mass of darker shade than the gray background. He called the trapper.

"Caribou," said Rea instantly. "The vanguard of the migration. Hear the Indians! Hear their cry: *'Aton! Aton! Aton!* They mean reindeer. The idiots have scared the herd with their infernal racket, an' no meat will they get. The caribou will keep to the ice, an' man or Indian can't stalk them there."

For a few moments his companion surveyed the lake and shore with a plainsman's eye, then dashed within to reappear with a Winchester in each hand. Through the crowd of bewailing, bemoaning Indians he sped, to the low, dying bank. The hard crust of snow upheld him. The gray cloud was a thousand yards out upon the lake and moving southeast. If the caribou did not swerve from this course they would pass close to a projecting point of land, half mile up the lake. So, keeping a wary eye upon them, the hunter ran swiftly. He had not hunted antelope and buffalo on the plains all his life without learning how to approach moving game. As long as the caribou were in action, they could not tell whether he moved or was motionless. In order to tell if an object was inanimate or not, they must stop to see, of which fact the keen hunter took advantage. Suddenly he saw the gray mass slow down and bunch up. He stopped running, to stand like a stump. When the reindeer moved again, he moved, and when they slackened again, he stopped and became motionless. As they kept to their course, he worked gradually closer and closer. Soon he distinguished gray, bobbing heads. When the leader showed signs of halting in his slow trot the hunter again became a statue. He saw they were easy to deceive; and, daringly confident of success, he encroached on the ice and closed up the gap till not more than two hundred yards separated him from the gray, bobbing, antlered mass.

Jones dropped on one knee. A moment only his eyes lingered

admiringly on the wild and beautiful spectacle; then he swept one of the rifles to a level. Old habit made the little beaded sight cover first the stately leader. Bang. The gray monarch leaped straight forward, forehoofs up, antlered head back, to fall dead with a crash. Then for a few moments, the Winchester spat a deadly stream of fire, and when emptied was thrown down for the other gun, which in the steady, sure hands of the hunter, belched death to the caribou.

The herd rushed on, leaving the white surface of the lake gray with a struggling, kicking, bellowing heap. When Jones reached the caribou, he saw several trying to rise on crippled legs. With his knife he killed these, not without some hazard to himself. Most of the fallen ones were already dead, and the others soon lay still. Beautiful gray creatures they were, almost white, with wide-reaching, symmetrical horns.

A medley of yells arose from the shore, and Rea appeared running with two sleds, with the whole tribe of Yellow Knives pouring out of the forest behind him.

"Buff, you're jest what old Jim said you was," thundered Rea, as he surveyed the gray pile. "Here's winter meat, an' I'd not given a biscuit for all the meat I thought you'd get."

"Thirty shots in less than thirty seconds!" said Jones, "an' I'll bet every ball I sent touched hair. How many reindeer?"

"Twenty! Twenty, Buff, or I've forgot how to count. I guess mebbe you can handle them shootin' arms. Ho! here comes the howlin' redskins."

Rea whipped out a bowie knife and began disemboweling the reindeer. He had not proceeded far in his task when the crazed savages were around him. Every one carried a basket or receptacle, which he swung aloft, and they sang, prayed, rejoiced on their knees. Jones turned away from the sickening scenes that convinced him these savages were little better than cannibals. Rea cursed them, and tumbled them over, and threatened them with the big bowie. An altercation ensued, heated on his side, frenzied on theirs. Thinking some treachery might befall his comrade, Jones ran into the thick of the group.

"Share with them, Rea, share with them."

Whereupon the giant hauled out ten smoking carcasses. Bursting into a babble of savage glee and tumbling over one another, the Indians pulled the caribou to the shore.

"Thievin' fools!" growled Rea, wiping the sweat from his brow. "Said they'd prevailed on the Great Spirit to send the reindeer. Why, they'd never've smelled warm meat but for you. Now, Buff, they'll gorge every hair, hide an' hoof of their share in less than a week. That's the last we do for the damned cannibals. Didn't you see them eatin' of the raw innards? Faugh! I'm calculatin' we'll see no more reindeer. It's late for the migration. The big herd has driven southward. But we're lucky, thanks to your prairie trainin'. Come on now with the sleds, or we'll have a pack of wolves to fight."

By loading the reindeers on each sled, the hunters were not long in transporting them to the cabin. "Buff, there ain't much doubt about them keepin' nice and cool," said Rea. "They'll freeze, an' we can skin them when we want."

That night the starved wolf dogs gorged themselves till they could not rise from the snow. Likewise the Yellow Knives feasted. How long the reindeer might have served the wasteful tribe, Rea and Jones never found out. The next day two Indians arrived with dog trains, and their advent was hailed with another feast, and a pow-wow that lasted into the night.

"Guess we're goin' to get rid of our blasted hungry neighbors," said Rea, coming in next morning with the water pail, "an' I'll be durned, Buff, if I don't believe them crazy heathens have been told about you. Them Indians was messengers. Grab your gun, an' let's walk over and see."

The Yellow Knives were breaking camp, and the hunters were at once conscious of the difference in their bearing. Rea addressed several braves, but got no reply. He laid his broad hand on the old wrinkled chief, who repulsed him, and turned his back. With a growl, the trapper turned the Indian round, and spoke as many words of the language as he knew. He got a cold response, which ended in the ragged old chief starting up, stretching a long, dark arm northward and with eyes fixed in fanatical subjection, shouting: *"Naza! Naza! Naza!"*

"Heathen!" Rea shook his gun in the faces of the messengers. "It'll go bad with you to come Nazain' any longer on our trail. Come, Buff, clear out before I get mad."

When they were once more in the cabin, Rea told Jones that the messengers had been sent to warn the Yellow Knives not to aid the white hunters in any way. That night the dogs were kept inside, and the men took turns in watching. Morning showed a broad trail southward. And with the going of the Yellow Knives the mercury dropped to fifty, and the long twilight winter night fell.

So with this agreeable riddance and plenty of meat and fuel to cheer them, the hunters sat down in their snug cabin to wait many months for daylight.

Those few intervals when the wind did not blow were the only times Rea and Jones got out of doors. To the plainsman, new to the north, the dim gray world about him was of exceeding interest. Out of the twilight shone a wan, round, lusterless ring that Rea said was the sun. The silence and desolation were heart-numbing.

"Where are the wolves?" asked Jones of Rea.

"Wolves can't live on snow. They're farther south after caribou, or farther north after musk-ox.

In those few still intervals Jones remained out as long as he dared, with the mercury sinking to sixty degrees. He turned from the wonder of the unreal, remote sun, to the marvel in the north—Aurora borealis—ever-present, ever-changing, ever-beautiful! and he gazed in rapt attention.

"Polar lights," said Rea, as if he were speaking of biscuits. "You'll freeze. It's gettin' cold."

Cold it became, to the matter of seventy degrees. Frost covered the walls of the cabin and the roof, except just over the fire. The reindeer were harder than iron. A knife or an ax or a steel trap burned as if it had been heated in fire, and stuck to the hand. The hunters experienced trouble in breathing; the air hurt their lungs.

The months dragged. Rea grew more silent day by day, and as he sat before the fire his wide shoulders sagged lower and lower. Jones, unaccustomed to the waiting, the restraint, the barrier of the north, worked on guns, sleds, harness, till he felt he would go mad. Then to save his mind he constructed a windmill of caribou hides and pondered over it trying to invent, to put into practical use an idea he had once conceived.

Hour after hour he lay under his blankets unable to sleep, and listened to the north wind. Sometimes Rea mumbled in his slumbers; once his giant form started up, and he muttered a woman's name. Shadows from the fire flickered on the walls, visionary, spectral shadows, cold and gray, fitting the north. At such times he longed with all the power of his soul to be among those scenes far southward, which he called home. For days, Rea never spoke a word, only gazed into the fire, ate and slept. Jones, drifting far from his real self, feared the strange mood of the trapper and sought to break it, but without avail. More and more he reproached himself, and singularly on the one fact that, as he did not smoke himself, he had brought only a small store of tobacco. Rea, inordinate and inveterate smoker, had puffed away all the weed in clouds of white, then had relapsed into gloom.

III

At last the marvel in the north dimmed, the obscure gray shade lifted, the hope in the south brightened, and the mercury climbed—reluctantly, with a tyrant's hate to relinquish power.

Spring weather at twenty-five below zero! On April 12th, a small band of Indians made their appearance. Of the Dog were

they, an offcast of the Great Slaves, according to Rea, and as
motley, staring and starved as the Yellow Knives. But they were
friendly, which presupposed ignorance of the white hunters, and
Rea persuaded the strongest brave to accompany them as guide
northward after musk-oxen.

On April 16th, having given the Indians several caribou
carcasses, and assuring them that the cabin was protected by
white spirits, Rea and Jones, each with sled and train of dogs,
started out after their guide, who was similarly equipped, over the
glistening snow toward the north. They made sixty miles the first
day, and pitched their Indian tipi on the shores of Artillery Lake.
Travelling northeast, they covered its white waste of one hundred
miles in two days. Then a day due north, over a rolling,
monotonously snowy plain, devoid of rock, tree, or shrub, brought
them into a country of the strangest, queerest little spruce trees,
very slender, and none of them over fifteen feet in height. A
primeval forest of sapplings.

"Ditchen Nechila!" said the guide.

"Land of the sticks little," said Rea.

An occasional reindeer was seen, and numerous fox and hares
trotted off into the woods, evincing more curiosity than fear. All
were silver white, even the reindeer, at a distance, taking the hue
of the north. Once a beautiful creature, unblemished as the snow
it trod, ran up a ridge and stood watching the hunters. It
resembled a monster dog, only it was inexpressibly more
wild-looking.

"Ho! Ho! there you are!" cried Rea, reaching for his
Winchester. "Polar wolf! Them's the white devils we'll have hell
with."

As if the wolf understood, he lifted his white, sharp head and
uttered a bark or howl that was like nothing so much as a
haunting, unearthly mourn. The animal then merged into the
white, as if he were really a spirit of the world whence his cry
seemed to come.

In this ancient forest of youthful-appearing trees, the hunters cut firewood to the full carrying capacity of the sleds. For five days, the Indian guide drove his dogs over the smooth crust, and on the sixth day, about noon, halting in a hollow, he pointed to tracks in the snow and called out, *"Ageter! Ageter! Ageter!"*

The hunters saw sharply defined hoof marks, not unlike the tracks of reindeer, except that they were longer. The tipi was set up on the spot and the dogs unharnessed.

The Indian led the way with the dogs, and Rea and Jones followed, slipping over the hard crust without sinking in and travelling swiftly. Soon the guide, pointing, again let out the cry *"Ageter!"* at the same moment loosing the dogs.

Some few hundred yards down the hollow, a number of large black animals, not unlike the shaggy, humpy buffalo, lumbered over the snow. Jones echoed Rea's yell, and broke into a run, easily distancing the puffing giant.

The musk-oxen squared round to the dogs and were soon surrounded by the yelping pack. Jones came up to find six old bulls uttering grunts of rage and shaking ram-like horns at their tormentors. Notwithstanding that for Jones this was the culmination of years of desire, the crowning moment, the climax and fruition of long harbored dreams, he halted before the tame and helpless beasts, with joy not unmixed with pain.

"It will be murder!" he exclaimed. "It's like shooting down sheep."

Rea came crashing up behind him and yelled: "Get busy. We need fresh meat, an' I want the skins."

The bulls succumbed to well-directed shots, and the Indian and Rea hurried back to camp with the dogs to fetch the sleds, while Jones examined with warm interest the animals he had wanted to see all his life. He found the largest bull approached within a third of the size of a buffalo. He was of a brownish-black color and very like a large, wooly ram. His head was broad, with sharp, small ears; the horns had wide and flattened bases and lay flat on

the head, to run down back of the eyes, then curve forward to a
sharp point. Like the bison, the musk-ox had short, heavy limbs,
covered with very long hair, and small, hard hoofs with hairy
tufts inside the curve of bone, which probably served as pads or
checks to hold the hoof firm on ice. His legs seemed out of
proportion to his body.

Two musk-oxen were loaded on a sled and hauled to camp in
one trip. Skinning them was but short work for such expert
hands. All the choice cuts of meat were saved. No time was lost in
broiling a steak, which they found sweet and juicy, with a flavor of
musk that was disagreeable.

"Now, Rea, for the calves," exclaimed Jones, "and then we're
homeward bound."

"I hate to tell this redskin," replied Rea. "He'll be like the
others. But it ain't likely he'd desert us here. He's far from his
base, with nothin' but thet old musket." Rea then commanded the
attention of the brave, and began to mangle the Great Slave and
Yellow Knife languages. Of this mixture Jones knew but a few
words. "Ageter nechila," which Rea kept repeating, he knew,
however, meant "musk-oxen little."

The guide stared, suddenly appeared to get Rea's meaning,
then vigorously shook his head and gazed at Jones in fear and
horror. Following this came an action as singular and inexplicable.
Slowly rising, he faced the north, lifted his hand, and remained
statuesque in his immobility. Then he began deliberately packing
his blankets and traps on his sled, which had not been unhitched
from the train of dogs.

"Jackoway ditchen hula," he said, and pointed south.

"Jackoway ditchen hula," echoed Rea. "The damned Indian
says 'wife sticks none.' He's goin' to quit us. What do you think of
thet? His wife's out of wood. *Jackoway* out of wood, an' here we
are two days from the Arctic Ocean! Jones, the damned heathen
don't go back!"

The trapper cooly cocked his rifle. The savage, who plainly saw
and understood the action, never flinched. He turned his breast to

Rea, and there was nothing in his demeanor to suggest his relation to a craven tribe.

"Good heavens, Rea, don't kill him! exclaimed Jones, knocking up the levelled rifle.

"Why not, I'd like to know?" demanded Rea, as if he were considering the fate of a threatening beast. "I reckon it'd be a bad thing for us to let him go."

"Let him go," said Jones. "We are here on the ground. We have dogs and meat. We'll get our calves and reach the lake as soon as he does, and we might get there before."

"Mebbee we will," growled Rea.

No vacillation attended the Indian's mode. From a friendly guide, he had suddenly been transformed into a dark, sullen savage. He refused the musk-ox meat offered by Jones, and he pointed south and looked at the white hunters as if he asked them to go with him. Both men shook their heads in answer. The savage struck his breast a resounding blow and with his index finger pointed at the white of the north, he shouted dramatically: *"Naza! Naza! Naza!"*

He then leaped upon his sled, lashed his dogs into a run, and without looking back disappeared over a ridge.

The musk-ox hunters sat long silent. Finally Rea shook his shaggy locks and roared. "Ho! Ho! *Jackoway* out of wood! *Jackoway* out of wood!"

On the day following the desertion, Jones found tracks to the north of the camp, making a broad trail in which were numerous little imprints that sent him flying back to get Rea and the dogs. Musk-oxen in great numbers had passed in the night, and Jones and Rea had not trailed the herd a mile before they had it in sight. When the dogs burst into full cry, the musk-oxen climbed a high knoll and squared about to give battle.

"Calves! Calves! Calves!" cried Jones.

"Hold back! Hold back! Thet's a big herd, an' they'll show fight."

As good fortune would have it, the herd split up into several sections, and one part, hard pressed by the dogs, ran down the knoll, to be cornered under the lee of a bank. The hunters, seeing this small number, hurried upon them to find three cows and five badly frightened little calves backed against the bank of snow, with small red eyes fastened on the barking, snapping dogs.

To a man of Jones's experience and skill, the capturing of the calves was a ridiculously easy piece of work. The cows tossed their heads, watched the dogs, and forgot their young. The first cast of the lasso settled over the neck of a little fellow. Jones hauled him out over the slippery snow and laughed as he bound the hairy legs. In less time than he had taken to capture one buffalo calf, with half the effort, he had all the little musk-oxen bound fast. Then he signalled this feat by pealing out an Indian yell of victory.

"Buff, we've got 'em," cried Rea; "an' now for the hell of it—gettin' 'em home. I'll fetch the sleds. You might as well down the best cow for me. I can use another skin."

Of all Jones's prizes of captured wild beasts—which numbered nearly every species common to western North America—he took greatest pride in the little musk-oxen. In truth, so great had been his passion to capture some of these rare and inaccessible mammals, that he considered the day's work the fulfillment of his life's purpose. He was happy. Never had he been so delighted as when, the very evening of their captivity, the musk-oxen, evincing no particular fear of him began to dig with sharp hoofs into the snow for moss. And they found moss, and ate it, which solved Jones's greatest problem. He had hardly dared to think how to feed them, and here they were picking sustenance out of the frozen snow.

"Rea, will you look at that! Rea, will you look at that!" he kept repeating. "See, they're hunting feed."

And the giant, with his rare smile, watched him play with the calves. They were about two and a half feet high, and resembled long haired sheep. The ears and horns were undiscernible, and their color considerably lighter than that of the matured beasts.

"No sense of fear of man," said the life-student of animals. "But they shrink from the dogs."

In packing for the journey south, the captives were strapped on the sleds. This circumstance necessitated a sacrifice of meat and wood, which brought grave, doubtful shakes of Rea's great head.

Days of hastening over the icy snow, with short hours for sleep and rest, passed before the hunters awoke to the consciousness that they were lost. The meat they had packed had gone to feed themselves and the dogs. Only a few sticks of wood were left.

"Better kill a calf, an' cook meat while we've got a little wood left," suggested Rea.

"Kill one of my calves? I'd starve first!" cried Jones.

The hungry giant said no more.

They headed southwest. All about them glared the grim monotony of the arctics. No rock or bush or tree made a welcome mark upon the hoary plain Wonderland of frost, white marble desert, infinitude of gleaming silences.

Snow began to fall, making the dogs flounder, obliterating the sun by which they travelled. They camped to wait for clearing weather. Biscuits soaked in tea made their meal. At dawn Jones crawled out of the tipi. The snow had ceased, but where were the dogs? He yelled in alarm. Then the little mounds of white, scattered here and there, became animated, heaved, rocked and rose to fall to pieces, exposing the dogs. Blankets of snow had been their covering.

Rea had ceased his "*Jackoway* out of wood," for a reiterated question: "Where are the wolves?"

"Lost," replied Jones in hollow humor.

Near the close of that day in which they had resumed travel, from the crest of a ridge they described a long, low, undulating dark line. It proved to be the forest of "little sticks," where, with grateful assurance of fire and of soon finding their old trail, they made camp.

"We've four biscuits left, an' enough tea for one drink each," said Rea. "I calculate we're two hundred miles from Great Slave Lake. Where are the wolves?"

At that moment the night wind wafted through the forest a long, haunting mourn. The calves shifted uneasily; the dogs raised sharp noses to sniff the air, and Rea, settling back against a tree, cried out: "Ho! Ho!" Again the savage sound, a keen wailing note with the hunger of the northland in it, broke the cold silence. "You'll see a pack of real wolves in a minute," said Rea. Soon a swift pattering of feet down a forest slope brought him to his feet with a curse to reach a brawny hand for his rifle. White streaks crossed the black of the tree trunks; then indistinct forms, the color of snow, swept up, spread out and streaked to and fro. Jones thought the great, gaunt, pure white beasts the spectral wolves of Rea's fancy, for they were silent, and silent wolves must belong to dreams only.

"Ho! Ho!" yelled Rea. "There's green-fire eyes for you, Buff. Hell itself ain't nothin' to these white devils. Get the calves in the tipi, an' stand ready to loose the dogs, for we've got to fight."

Raising his rifle he opened fire upon the white foe. A struggling, rustling sound followed the shots. But whether it was the threshing of wolves dying in agony, or the fighting of the fortunate ones over those shot, could not be ascertained in the confusion.

Following the example Jones also fired rapidly on the other side of the tipi. The same inarticulate, silently rustling wrestle succeeded this volley.

"Wait!" cried Rea. "Be sparin' of cartridges."

The dogs strained at their chains and bravely bayed the wolves. The hunters heaped logs and brush on the fire, which, blazing up, sent a bright light far into the woods. On the outer edge of that circle moved the white, restless, gliding forms.

"They're more afraid of fire than of us," said Jones.

So it proved. When the fire burned and crackled they kept well in the background. The hunters had a long respite from serious anxiety, during which time they collected all the available wood at hand. But at midnight, when this had been mostly consumed, the wolves grew bold again.

"Have you any shots left for the 45-90, besides what's in the magazine?" asked Rea.

"Yes, a good handful."

"Well, get busy."

With careful aim Jones emptied the magazine into the gray, gliding, groping mass. The same rustling, shuffling, almost silent strife ensued.

"Rea, there's something uncanny about those brutes. A silent pack of wolves."

"Ho! Ho!" rolled the giant's answer through the woods.

For the present, the attack appeared to have been effectually checked. The hunters, sparingly adding a little of their fast diminishing pile of fuel to the fire, decided to lie down for much needed rest, but not for sleep. How long they lay there, cramped by the calves, listening for stealthy steps, neither could tell; it might have been moments and it might have been hours. All at once came a rapid rush of pattering feet, succeeded by a chorus of angry barks, then a terrible commingling of savage snarls, growls, snaps and yelps.

"Out!" yelled Rea. "They're on the dogs!"

Jones pushed his cocked rifle ahead of him and straightened up outside the tipi. A wolf, large as a panther and white as the gleaming snow, sprang at him. Even as he discharged his rifle, right against the breast of the beast, he saw its dripping jaws, its wicked green eyes, like spurts of fire and felt its hot breath. It fell at his feet and writhed in the death struggle. Slender bodies of black and white, whirling and tussling together, sent out fiendish uproar. Rea threw a blazing stick of wood among them, which sizzled as it met the furry coats, and brandishing another he ran into the thick of the fight. Unable to stand the proximity of fire, the wolves bolted and loped off into the woods.

"What a huge brute!" exclaimed Jones, dragging the one he had shot into the light. It was a superb animal, thin, supple, strong, with a coat of frosty fur, very long and fine. Rea began at once to skin it, remarking that he hoped to find other pelts in the morning.

Though the wolves remained in the vicinity of camp, none ventured near. The dogs moaned and whined; their restlessness increased as dawn approached, and when the gray light came, Jones found that some of them had been badly lacerated by the fangs of the wolves. Rea hunted for dead wolves and found not so much as a piece of white fur.

Soon the hunters were speeding southward. Other than a disposition to fight among themselves, the dogs showed no evil effects of the attack. They were lashed to their best speed, for Rea said the white rangers of the north would never quit their trail. All day the men listened for the wild, lonesome, haunting mourn, but it came not.

A wonderful halo of white and gold, that Rea called a sundog, hung in the sky all afternoon, and dazzlingly bright over the dazzling world of snow, circled and glowed a mocking sun, brother of the desert mirage, beautiful illusion, smiling cold out of the polar blue.

The first pale evening star twinkled in the east when the hunters made camp on the shore of Artillery Lake. At dusk the clear, silent air opened to the sound of a long, haunting mourn.

"Ho! Ho!" called Rea. His hoarse, deep voice rang defiance to the foe.

While he built a fire before the tipi, Jones strode up and down, suddenly to whip out his knife and make for the tame little musk-oxen, now digging in the snow. Then he wheeled abruptly and held out the blade to Rea.

"What for?" demanded the giant.

"We've got to eat," said Jones. "And I can't kill one of them. I can't, so you do it."

"Kill one of our calves?" snorted Rea. "Not till hell freezes over! I ain't commenced to get hungry. Besides, the wolves are going to eat us, calves and all."

Nothing more was said. They ate their last biscuit. Jones packed the calves away in the tipi, and turned to the dogs. All day they had worried him; something was amiss with them, and even as he went among them a fierce fight broke out. Jones saw it was unusual, for the attacked dogs showed craven fear, and the attacking ones a howling, savage intensity that surprised him. Then one of the vicious brutes rolled his eyes, frothered at the mouth, shuddered and leaped in his harness, vented a hoarse howl and fell back shaking and retching.

"My God! Rea!" cried Jones in horror. "Come here! Look! That dog is dying of rabies! Hydrophobia! The white wolves have hydrophobia!"

"If you ain't right!" exclaimed Rea. "I seen a dog die of that once, an' he acted like this. An' thet one ain't all. Look, Buff! look at them green eyes! Didn't I say the white wolves was hell? We'll have to kill every dog we've got."

Jones shot the dog, and soon afterward three more that manifested signs of the disease. It was an awful situation. To kill all the dogs meant simply to sacrifice his life and Rea's; it meant abandoning hope of ever reaching the cabin. Then to risk being bitten by one of the poisoned, maddened brutes, to risk the most horrible of agonizing deaths that was even worse.

"Rea, we've one chance," cried Jones, with pale face. "Can you hold the dogs, one by one, while I muzzle them?"

"Ho! Ho!" replied the giant. Placing his bowie knife between his teeth, with gloved hands he seized and dragged one of the dogs to the campfire. The animal whined and protested, but showed no ill spirit. Jones muzzled his jaws tightly with strong cords. Another and another were tied up, then one which tried to snap at Jones was nearly crushed by the giant's grip. The last, a surly brute, broke out into mad ravings the moment he felt the touch of Jones's hands, and writhing and frothing, he snapped at his sleeve. Rea jerked him loose and held him in the air with one arm, while with the other he swung the bowie. They hauled the dead dogs out on the snow, and returning to the fire sat down to await the cry they expected.

Presently, as darkness fastened down tight, it came—the same cry, wild, haunting, mourning. But for hours it was not repeated.

"Better rest some," said Rea; "I'll call you if they come."

Jones dropped to sleep as he touched his blankets. Morning dawned for him, to find the great, dark, shadowy figure of the giant nodding over the fire.

"How's this? Why didn't you call me?" demanded Jones.

"The wolves only fought a little over the dead dogs."

On the instant, Jones saw a wolf skulking up the bank. Throwing up his rifle, which he had carried out of the tipi, he took a snap shot at the beast. It ran off on three legs, to go out of sight over the bank. Jones scrambled up the steep, slippery place, and upon arriving at the ridge, which took several moments of hard work, he looked everywhere for the wolf. In a moment he saw the animal, standing still some hundred or more paces down a hollow. With the quick report of Jones's second shot, the wolf fell and rolled over. The hunter ran to the spot to find the wolf was dead. Taking hold of a front paw, he dragged the animal over the snow to camp. Rea began to skin the animal, when suddenly he exclaimed:

"This fellow's hind foot is gone."

"That's strange. I saw it hanging by the skin as the wolf ran up the bank. I'll look for it."

By the bloody trail on the snow he returned to the place where the wolf had fallen, and thence back to the spot where its leg had been broken by the bullet. He discovered no sign of the foot.

"Didn't find it, did you?" asked Rea.

"No, and it appears odd to me. The snow is so hard the foot could not have sunk."

"Well, the wolf ate his foot, thet's what," returned Rea. "Look at them teeth marks!"

"Is it possible?" Jones stared at the leg Rea held up.

"Yes it is. These wolves are crazy at times. You've seen thet. An' the smell of blood, an' nothin' else, mind you, in my opinion, made him eat his own foot. We'll cut him open."

Impossible as the thing seemed to Jones—and he could not but believe further evidence of his own eyes—it was even stranger to drive a train of mad dogs. Yet that was what Rea and he did, and lashed them, beat them to cover many miles in the long day's journey. Rabies had broken out in several dogs so alarmingly that Jones had to kill them at the end of the run. And hardly had the sound of the shots died, when faint and far away, but clear as a bell, bayed on the wind the same haunting mourn of a trailing wolf.

"Ho! Ho! where are the wolves?" cried Rea.

A waiting, watching, sleepless night followed. Again the hunters faced the south. Hour after hour, riding, running, walking, they urged the poor, jaded, poisoned dogs. At dark, they reached the head of Artillery Lake. Rea placed the tipi between two huge stones. Then the hungry hunters, tired, grim, silent, desperate, awaited the familiar cry.

It came on the cold wind, the same haunting mourn, dreadful in its significance.

Absence of fire inspired the wary wolves. Out of the pale gloom gaunt white forms emerged, agile and stealthy, slipping on velvet padded feet, closer, closer, closer. The dogs wailed in terror.

"Into the tipi!" yelled Rea.

Jones plunged in after his comrade. The despairing howls of the dogs, drowned in more savage, frightful sounds, knelled one tragedy and foreboded a more terrible one. Jones looked out to see a white mass, like leaping waves of a rapid.

"Pump lead into them," cried Rea.

Rapidly, Jones emptied his rifle into the white fray. The mass split; gaunt wolves leaped high to fall back dead; others wriggled and limped away; others dragged their hind quarters; others darted at the tipi.

"No more cartridges!" yelled Jones.

The giant grabbed the ax, and barred the door of the tipi. Crash! the heavy iron cleaved the skull of the first brute. Crash! it lamed the second. Then Rea stood in the narrow passage between the rocks, waiting with uplifted ax. A shaggy, white demon, snapping his jaws, sprang like a dog. A sodden, thudding blow met him and he slunk away without a cry. Another rabid beast launched his white body at the giant. Like a flash, the ax descended. In agony, the wolf fell, to spin round and round, running on his hind legs, while his head and shoulders and forelegs remain in the snow. His back was broken.

Jones crouched in the opening of the tipi, knife in hand. He doubted his senses. This was a nightmare. He saw two wolves leap at once. He heard the crash of the ax; he saw one wolf go down and the other slip under the swinging weapon to grasp the giant's hip. Jones heard the rend of cloth, and then he pounced like a cat, to drive his knife into the body of the beast. Another nimble foe lunged at Rea, to sprawl broken and limp from the iron. It was silent fight. The giant shut the way to his comrade and the calves; he made no outcry; he needed but one blow for every beast; magnificent, he wielded death and faced it—silent. He brought the white, wild dogs of the north down with lightning blows, and when no more sprang to the attack, down on the frigid silence he rolled his cry: "Ho! Ho!"

"Rea! Rea! how is it with you?" called Jones, climbing out.

"A torn coat—no more, my lad!"

Three of the poor dogs were dead; the fourth and last gasped at the hunters and died.

The wintry night became a thing of half-conscious past, a dream to the hunters, manifesting its reality only by the stark, stiff bodies of wolves, white in the gray morning.

"If we can eat, we'll make the cabin," said Rea. "But the dogs an' wolves are poison."

"Shall I kill a calf?" asked Jones.

"Ho! Ho! when hell freezes over—if we must!"

Jones found one 45-90 cartridge in all the outfit and with that in the chamber of the rifle, once more struck south. Spruce trees began to show on the barrens and caribou trails roused hope in the hearts of the hunters.

"Look! in the spruces," whispered Jones, dropping the rope of his sled. Among the black trees gray objects moved.

"Caribou!" said Rea. "Hurry! Shoot! Don't miss!"

But Jones waited. He knew the value of the last bullet. He had a hunter's patience. When the caribou came out in an open space, Jones whistled. It was then the rifle grew set and fixed; it was then the red fire belched forth.

At four hundred yards, the bullet took some fraction of time to strike. What a long time that was! Then both hunters heard the spiteful spat of the lead. The caribou fell, jumped up, ran down the slope, and fell again to rise no more.

An hour of rest, with fire and meat, changed the world to the hunters; still glistening, it yet had lost its bitter cold, its deathlike clutch.

"What's this?" cried Jones.

Moccasin tracks of different sizes, all toeing north, arrested the hunters.

"Pointed north! Wonder what thet means?" Rea plodded on, doubtfully shaking his head.

Night again, clear, cold, silver, starlit, silent night! The hunters rested, listening ever for the haunting mourn. Dawn again, white, passionless, monotonous, silent day! The hunters travelled on— on—ever listening for the haunting mourn of the wolves.

Another dusk found them within thirty miles of their cabin. Only one more day now.

Rea talked of his furs, of the splendid white furs he could not bring. Jones talked of his little musk-oxen calves and joyfully watched them dig for moss in the snow.

Vigilance relaxed that night. Outworn nature rebelled, and both hunters slept.

Rea awoke first, and kicking off the blankets, went out. His terrible roar of rage made Jones fly to his side.

Under the very shadow of the tipi, where the little musk-oxen had been tethered, they lay stretched out pathetically on crimson snow—stiff, stone-cold, dead. Moccasin tracks told the story of the tragedy.

Jones leaned against his comrade.

The giant raised his huge fist.

"*Jackoway* out of wood! *Jackoway* out of wood!"

Then he choked.

The north wind, blowing through the thin, dark weird spruce trees, mounted and seemed to sigh, *"Naza! Naza! Naza!"*

Zane Grey feeding bears.